"Are you ready for ___

"Yes." She was calmer than when he had fetched her. Her life waited on the other side of this decision and she was ready to live it.

He kept his eyes on hers, she watched him slip a hand into his coat pocket and withdraw a black velvet box that he placed between them, pulling his hand away from hers to open the lid with a click.

And even though Lily knew this wasn't real, she couldn't breathe. Couldn't reach into the box and pluck that amazing ring out. And it was amazing. Timeless.

"Lily, marry me." It wasn't a question, wasn't a request. It was a statement convincing her that she could place her trust in him. Telling her that they were in this madness together.

"Yes," she choked, surprising herself at how easily the word fell out. Lily worried that it would be hard to say yes when the time came but it wasn't. For whatever reason, her *yes* felt right.

Julian pinched the ring out of the box and slid it onto her finger then brushed his lips across her knuckles. The world disappeared.

Bella Mason has been a bookworm from an early age. She has been regaling people with stories from the time she discovered she could hold the dinner table hostage with her reimagined fairy tales. After earning a degree in Journalism, she rekindled her love of writing and she now writes full-time. When she isn't imagining dashing heroes and strong heroines, she can be found exploring Melbourne, with her nose in a book or lusting after fast cars.

Books by Bella Mason

Harlequin Presents

Awakened by the Wild Billionaire

Visit the Author Profile page
at Harlequin.com.

Bella Mason

THEIR DIAMOND RING RUSE

Recycling programs for this product may not exist in your area.

ISBN-13: 978-1-335-59284-2

Their Diamond Ring Ruse

For questions and comments about the quality of this book, please contact us at CustomerService@Harlequin.com.

Harlequin Enterprises ULC
22 Adelaide St. West, 41st Floor
Toronto, Ontario M5H 4E3, Canada
www.Harlequin.com

Printed in U.S.A.

THEIR DIAMOND RING RUSE

For the crazy redhead in my life. Lindsay, this one's for you. You know why.

CHAPTER ONE

THIS ROOM HAD not changed in twenty years. From the books to the trinkets to the globe bar standing in the corner, everything was exactly as it had always been. And it made her feel like running.

Lily Barnes-Shah stood across the room from her brother, Devan. They'd used to love this room. Her father's office. Even though they'd never been allowed to play in here, somehow they always had. The dark wood furniture, massive carved desk and heavy drapes had provided endless hiding places for their epic hide and seek games. Her father would eventually find them and usher them out with a stern warning and a barely hidden smile.

Now it felt like a creepy monument.

And remembering that smile that had made her love her strict father so much brought mostly anger. As did her brother. Once her best friend, now she barely recognised the calculating man he'd become.

Her father Samar—Sam, as he'd been known—had passed away from a sudden heart attack a mere two months ago. Just weeks from his sixty-sixth birthday. Everything had changed for Lily that day. Her desperation had grown steadily since, and the one person she'd thought she could trust to help her was proving how little he cared.

It was a deep cut to her already aching heart.

Shah International had been passed down from their grandfather to their father, and now to Devan. And since he had joined their father in business she and Devan had grown steadily apart. All he focussed on was his work at the family company that dealt with everything from import and export and distribution to a series of chain store brands. Her father had got what he'd always wanted—his heir following in his footsteps—and she lost her best friend. Her brother.

'Dad planned all this years ago. You were fine with it then, so why is it a problem now?' Devan asked from behind the desk.

The drapes behind him were opened wide but the doors to the terrace were shut, and the hedge beyond was so tall that she couldn't see the blue San Francisco sky. God, he looked so much like their father. It took everything in her not to look away. They had the same golden-brown skin, dark brown eyes, thick black hair. He was the patriarch of the family now. His word was law.

'I was never fine with it, but what could I do? I was nineteen and studying abroad. I obeyed Dad, but still I begged, for five years!'

Lily had always wanted to please their father—had done everything she could to make him proud. He'd been a traditional man, and had expected obedience, but this arrangement was beyond what she could endure.

'I've been thinking about it a lot lately. The fact that Dad promised me he would find a way out. Well, Dad is dead now, Dev, so it's up to you. Only you can put a stop to this.'

That conversation with her father had been on repeat in her head. Yes, he was the one who had put her in this position, but he had given her hope that he would try to free her of the arrangement after he had seen how controlling Lincoln was. He'd promised her he would find a different way, and he'd never gone back on his promises.

Well, not unless a heart attack that no one had seen coming made him.

'Your engagement...'

Her temper flared. How could Devan try to dress up this madness as an *'engagement'*. She hadn't been asked. Hadn't said yes. This was being forced upon her. She wanted him to call it what it was. After all, she was the one being treated like a commodity.

'Arranged marriage,' she said through clenched teeth.

'Your engagement protects us both.'

It grated on her nerves that Devan, who knew her better than anyone, could ignore the way she felt. That he could see how angry she was and not care. It hurt. How had they gone from friends to this?

'It protects an investment. I thought my brother would want to protect *me*,' Lily said softly, the words slipping out before she had the chance to stop them.

She had hoped so hard that Devan might want to help her. But she could see now that the boy who had doted on her was gone.

'Lily, I am. This is what's best for us. Yes, Shah International is doing well, and is ours, but Arum Corp... Dad only owned thirty percent of that, and Arthur owned fifty—which was fine when Arthur was alive, and still fine when he died and Lincoln took over...'

'But not now that Dad's gone?'

Arthur Harrison had been her father's best friend. Both had come from old money. They had socialised in the same circles, gone to the same schools, and studied at the same Ivy League universities. They'd been more like brothers than friends and had remained so over many years. So when Arthur had approached Sam with the idea that they go into business together, it had been a no brainer.

They had started with a single bakery—a test to see how well they could work together—but they had grown it into a supermarket, then a chain, and following that the company had moved into goods production.

Sam had agreed to a lesser share in the company for a few reasons, but primarily because going into business with friends was something he'd usually advised against, and a smaller shareholding would lessen his risk. It had been Arthur's first enterprise started from scratch, and there had been no telling how well it would do or if it would succeed at all.

To preserve their friendship, they had agreed to make a buy-back of shares possible if the partnership didn't work out. And, in a plan to protect the business they were starting, once they'd attracted other shareholders they'd agreed to a clause that said any shareholder could be voted off the board and their shares bought back should he in any way bring the business into disrepute.

So thirty percent had suited Sam at the beginning. After all, his main priority had always been Shah International...until Arum grew into the giant it had become.

Lily had loved Arthur. Just like her father, he'd been a shrewd businessman. Formidable in the boardroom, but loving when it came to his family. Which was why his son Lincoln had been such a surprise.

'Lincoln is the majority shareholder, Lil,' said Devan. 'We need you to marry him as planned and keep him happy. Keep him on good terms with us. He isn't his father. If I start buying back shares, it's going to sour the relationship. And you know he will find some way to implement that clause even if he has to fabricate a reason. We can't give him a chance to own eighty percent. What will happen to Arum then?'

'I don't want to marry him, Dev. I never did.' Lily felt nauseous. Beyond desperate now.

'I'm sorry, Lily. More than anyone, you and I know what Linc is like.'

How could they not? The three of them had grown up around each other. Devan had always been the responsible one. The leader of their group. When she was young, Lily had assumed it was simply because he was the eldest, and had thought it completely unfair. *She'd* wanted to be the leader, and thankfully Devan had always indulged her. She'd been a ball of energy. Making friends with everyone they'd met, always up for a game, but Lincoln... He had always been cold. Calculating. Spoilt and entitled. And it had only grown worse as they grew older.

When Sam and Arthur had joked about Lily and Lincoln getting married she had seen the look in his eyes. She knew the match wouldn't be because he wanted her—it would be because by tying himself to Lily, he would have complete control when the business fell to him and Devan. She would become a pawn he could use to control her brother.

After Arthur had died, Sam had approached Lincoln

to talk seriously about the possibility of a marriage. Because as much as he'd known Lincoln would benefit, her father had also known Lily and Devan would too. Devan had already shown a strategic mind, and Sam knew that with Lily binding the families together he would be able to leverage things to his benefit. Lincoln would be less likely to attempt to push out a member of his family.

Lily remembered well the day her father had told her of the marriage he wanted to arrange. The shudder that had run through her body. In that moment she had known how awful life with Lincoln would be.

'Yeah, foolish me for thinking you would want to spare your sister that,' she said now.

Unable to look at her brother any longer, she turned towards a shelf packed with books. Foolish was exactly what she felt, and she couldn't bear the thought of Devan seeing the hurt that would be written on her face.

Devan's voice softened. 'I don't want to force this on you, but it is what it is.'

She refused to look at him, and there was steel in her tone when she replied. 'So that's it? The company is more important than me?'

'Lily…' It was a reprimand.

Screw this.

Enough of trying to be polite. Trying to ask for help. She didn't need it. She had made something of herself without Devan—she didn't need him now.

'Don't *Lily* me, Dev. That's exactly how it is. You say Shah International is doing well? You and I both know that's an understatement. That company makes this family more money than it knows what to do with. So what if Lincoln tries to push you out of Arum? You'd barely feel the pinch. But all you all want is *more*, and you don't care that *I* am the one who will have to pay the price.'

'You don't know what you're talking about,' her brother said quietly. 'You have never wanted anything to do with the company.'

That was true. She had no interest in working in a glass tower every day. The corporate life had never appealed to her. Which was fine, because all that expectation had fallen on Devan, who had welcomed it.

Instead, her father had indulged her in her dream. He had paid for her to attend pastry school in France, and she had managed to earn a business degree while doing so. She had used both to start her patisserie on Fisherman's Wharf and now, at only twenty-four, she was running one of the most popular eateries in San Francisco.

That didn't mean she knew nothing of the family company.

She huffed a laugh. 'What happened to us, Dev? The old you would never have said that, because it isn't true, but this new version of you…this one looking down his nose at me…? I don't know him, and I don't care for him.'

Lily stalked towards the desk, where he was still seated.

'You're right, I didn't want to work in the company. And looking at what you've become, why would I? But I still know what it's worth. You need to see that you're so hung up on that thirty percent of Arum that you won't even consider the wealth you already have with Shah, even if it costs you your blood.'

'So if you don't get your way you're threatening to cut all ties with me? Throw me to the wolves?' he asked.

Lily took a deep breath. Just the thought of letting go of her brother cracked her soul. The fact that their relationship had become so contentious was a constant ache in her gut. All they had was each other. After their father's funeral, their mother had announced that she couldn't live in the big house in Presidio Heights with all the memories it contained. But she couldn't let it go either. So she'd decided to travel. The last Lily had heard from Victoria Barnes-Shah, she'd been somewhere in Italy.

That was another conversation Lily wanted to forget. She had confided in her mother about not wanting to marry Lincoln, but Victoria had urged her to do so regardless—because, as she had put it, *'Your father loved you so much, and he only wanted the best for his children. You should obey his wishes.'*

Maybe that had come from a place of grief, but all it had done was make Lily feel more alone.

And that had left her and Devan in this giant house with all the silence between them.

'I wish you could see how unfair it is even to ask me that.' She stared unflinchingly at him. 'I'd never intentionally hurt you, but if you won't help me I'll find a way to fix things on my own.'

His expression became concerned. 'Don't do anything rash, please.'

She refused to respond to that. She would do whatever she needed to. All she wanted was a chance to live her life freely. Marry someone she chose—if she chose to marry at all.

'And don't forget we have that networking event to-night,' Devan reminded her.

'You have got to be joking!' Lily snapped. 'After everything I've said?'

Devan heaved a sigh. 'Look, if you don't want to go with Lincoln, you don't have to. Just attend with me.'

Lily studied her brother, unsure if she could trust his invitation—and wasn't that just a kick in the teeth? But it occurred to her that it could be an olive branch, so she would take it.

'Fine.'

But that didn't mean she wasn't going to work on a way out from this very moment…

CHAPTER TWO

SEATED BESIDE HER BROTHER, Lily toyed with her diamond bracelet as she looked out through the window of the limousine. She hadn't said a word to Devan after their chat earlier, and the atmosphere between them was still tense.

They drove in utter silence through the tree-lined streets until the Bay came into view in utter silence save for the soft crooning Devan preferred lilting through the speakers. She had nothing more to say to her brother, but if she was being honest she was grateful that he hadn't forced her to attend this event with Lincoln.

'Can you pretend that you don't hate me when we walk in there?' Devan asked.

Lily glanced at him. His face was drawn into a frown. 'I don't hate you, Dev. I hate what everyone is making me do,' she said softly, and then turned back to stare out of the window.

Tonight was important, she knew. It was the first big business event since their father had died and Devan had taken over his role. She wanted to offer her support.

'You look nice, by the way,' he said after a brief pause.

Lily looked down at the pale yellow fabric of her

long, flowing designer dress, at her wrists cuffed in sparkling diamonds.

The event was being held at The Royal, a boutique hotel on The Presidio. Lily had always loved the place. It was beautiful in the day, but even more breathtaking at night, when the bridge was lit up. It was a small venue, close to the homes of those families with the most money.

As much as this was to be a business networking event, it was very clear who it was for. The tight-knit old money community that had begun this event many, many years ago. In fact, Lily knew only a few new people had ever made it in, and that was because their bank balances made them hard to ignore.

The limousine stopped under a portico. Instantly a young man in an impeccable uniform opened Lily's door and helped her step out.

As soon as they entered the large function room, lit by bright crystal lamps, Lily spotted the view of the Golden Gate Bridge, lit up and glowing against the inky sky, the Bay a glittering dark blue void beneath.

She felt Devan's hand between her shoulders, ushering her forward, and snapped her attention to all the formally dressed people in the room, dripping with wealth. Some held champagne or rich amber-coloured drinks in their hands. Others were gesturing animatedly with large smiles on their faces. The faint strains of classical music could be heard, though it was almost drowned out by the constant hum of voices.

Everywhere she looked there were groups of people, and in between, barely noticed, were black waistcoated waiters, circulating with trays of edible pieces of artistry.

She saw Devan scan the faces in the crowd before gesturing to her that they should head in one particular direction. Her stomach sank. She had hoped she would be able to spend the evening with her brother, despite their disagreement. Now she saw the impossibility of that. Felt hope die within her, only to be replaced by a burning anger she would have to cover up with a winning smile.

She turned to look at Devan and saw a flash of uncertainty in his eyes that quickly changed to a look of utter determination as he led her towards Lincoln Harrison. The bitter taste of betrayal coated her tongue. If it hadn't been clear to her this afternoon, it certainly was now: Devan was not going to help her.

Lily stared ahead of her at Lincoln, who had a look of sheer possessiveness in his eyes. He watched her as if she was a trinket that belonged to him, and in that moment that was how she felt. This was a business transaction and she was the commodity. It hurt.

She shook off her brother's touch. 'Hello, Lincoln.'

His blue eyes twinkled as he leaned in to kiss her, but she turned her face at the last moment, forcing his lips to press against her cheek. His blond hair brushed against her skin as he pulled away, his lips set in a grim line.

'Lily.' Lincoln slipped an arm around her waist, pulling her to his side.

His touch might as well have been a padlock and chain. That was how trapped she felt. She glared at her brother, but turned away. She couldn't look at either of them.

Her stomach roiled at the weight of Lincoln's hand on her hip. Not a sign of affection but a shackle. She couldn't breathe. Needed to get out of this place. Out of her life. Lincoln wanted them to wed in a year. How could she do that? How could she succumb to a life like that?

She couldn't. Would never survive it. Never survive being with this man who had asked her father if he *really* wanted to risk Devan's place at Arum when they had spoken once about calling off the arrangement. When Sam had tried to explain that Lily's goals no longer suited being married to him.

Bile rose in her throat when she thought of what freeing herself might mean for Devan. And she might displease her mother by going against her father's wishes, even though before he'd died he had promised to find a solution for her. But still she was stuck here.

Lily took a deep breath, trying to centre herself. To halt her panic and desperation to run. She needed to think, but when she opened her eyes a figure captured her attention. A man in a dark suit with red hair and no hint of a smile on his face.

He wasn't the tallest man in the room. Nor was he the largest or the brawniest. But he had a presence that shouted louder than any voice. It made him stand taller than anyone else. He had a predatory air that sucked all the attention away from everyone and everything else, focussing it all on him.

He was feral and beautiful, caged in a designer suit. But it didn't make him look trapped. No. It was the glossy coat of a jungle cat as it stalked its prey.

As if he felt her gaze on him he turned his eyes on her. While she couldn't tell the colour of them from where she stood, she felt a shiver pass through her, and even the constricting band of Lincoln's arm fell away.

* * *

Julian Ford stood at the bar, glass in hand. Raising the club soda and lime to his lips, he took a sip, rolling it around his tongue, relishing the tart bite. He hated these events, preferring to be at home or in his office, working. Growing his company or creating blueprints for new technology.

That wasn't an option tonight.

The exclusivity of this network was legendary. The only thing that had garnered him an invitation—and a reluctant one at that, he assumed—was his bank balance. No one would ignore a billionaire for too long. Especially one like him.

He hated having to make small talk with a bunch of rich snobs, but even he knew the importance of this kind of networking.

He glanced around the room once again, paying close attention to all the heads of industry he wished to win over. Mentally he sorted through the list of people who it would be most profitable for him to work with. To him, winning people over didn't mean playing nice and kissing ass. No. To Julian, winning meant making a success of the company he'd worked his hands to the bone to build. Winning meant showing people just what they would lose from *not* signing with him and how much they would gain from an association.

His attendance here was only the first step. What he needed was an in for the Zenith dinner in a few weeks' time. If this event was exclusive, it was nothing on the Zenith network. Much to his irritation, he had never yet received an invitation, and even his being here tonight didn't mean that was likely to change.

He took another sip of his drink, sliding his free hand into his pocket, and turned to face the older gentleman beside him, nursing a glass of Scotch as he ran his fingers through his salt-and-pepper hair.

'This turnout could work in your favour,' said Henry Cross, the man Julian owed so much to. He was his mentor. The one person in the world he trusted.

'I'm not interested in the numbers,' Julian replied.

'Of course not. I taught you better than that.' The old man smiled.

Julian had seen that smile so many times over the years, yet still he couldn't return it. Thankfully Henry never expected him to, which made being around him so much easier.

Julian had graduated from school early, which had meant he was far younger than anyone else at college. Far younger and far, far smarter. Henry had recognised the genius in a very poor, very serious, driven young man, and had taken him under his wing.

Now Julian owned IRES, a leader in renewable energy technology. His own invention—created while still a teenager—had made him a millionaire, and following that a billionaire, but the success of IRES had mostly come from overseas markets. He was still struggling to gain a foothold in the States.

It was hard to convince companies in the US to work with him when even those in San Francisco—the city in which he'd placed his headquarters—stubbornly refused to work with him. But his overseas success wasn't enough. Julian needed to replicate that success on home soil.

His drive to turn nothing into the behemoth IRES

now was had taken intelligence and an understanding of where exactly to focus his efforts. So, no, he would not be looking to get in bed with anyone in this room who had money—which was everyone—but the select few who would have the greatest impact.

After all, a predator didn't hunt an entire herd blindly…it selected its prey and went after it.

'You did,' he said now. 'The problem is I couldn't care less about the people who *want* to talk to me,' Julian added, looking around the room.

'That group will be hard to break into,' Henry agreed, glancing over his shoulder to the man Julian was looking at.

'Lincoln Harrison won't give me the time of day. He won't even take a call from IRES,' he said through clenched teeth.

'I heard a rumour that he's looking to invest in green energy for Arum…' Henry leaned against the bar.

'He is. But I'm betting he's hoping one of his associates with the correct pedigree will magically provide the solution he's looking for.'

This was the issue Julian kept crashing into. It didn't matter to people like Lincoln Harrison who could provide the best solution—what mattered was who from his approved list of old money sycophants could provide the best solution. Because in his world being born on the wrong side of the tracks was a blemish that couldn't be tolerated.

Just then a woman entered the function room. Skin golden-brown. Glossy black hair pinned up, exposing an elegant neck. Lithe and graceful, in a pale yellow dress that made him feel kissed by the sun. Such a change to the monochrome monotony in this room.

It was Lily Barnes-Shah.

And Julian couldn't look away as she and her brother Devan approached none other than Lincoln Harrison himself.

He watched with interest as she evaded his kiss, then stiffened at his touch.

Interesting.

With great effort Julian turned his attention back to Henry. It was hard to do, because everything in him wanted to keep looking at her.

'Why does he want to go green now? PR?' asked Henry.

'No...' Julian forced himself to pay attention to the conversation. 'And it's not out of moral responsibility either. He's found out how much money he would make in the long run, so he's prepared for the capital outlay now.'

'Well, as long as his money is good...'

Julian's gaze had started wandering back to Lily, but now it snapped back to his mentor. That wasn't all there was to it, but Julian didn't control his clients' motives, and as long as his own goals were being met he would have to be satisfied with that.

'That won't matter if I can't even get an in with Arum.'

'You know what the issue is, don't you?' said Henry.

Of course Julian knew, and he could do nothing about it.

'You're new money and your reputation. These people think you're too ruthless.'

His so-called ruthlessness followed him around constantly. For the most part Julian revelled in it, but occasionally it was a hindrance. He just always looked for the most efficient solution. Efficiency didn't leave time to care about feelings. Efficiency meant taking over companies, trimming away the fat, stripping it to its bare bones and then making it perform at its best.

Julian made things work. It was business. There should be no room for feelings. It wasn't logical. As for the other issue… There wasn't much he could do about that save marrying into that old money world. But marriage was not an option. *Ever.* Not with his past. His company and his money were good, and that would have to do.

'You need to show them a different side to you, Julian. Something they can relate to,' Henry continued.

'I'm not softening my edge just so that a bunch of elitist pricks can feel good about themselves. I'm the best at what I do. My work should stand alone.' Julian didn't raise his voice. He never let himself show anger. He could control himself. Had to.

'It should, but you'll catch a lot more flies with honey than with vinegar. Remember that. We'll talk more later—there's someone I need to see.'

Feeling someone's gaze boring into him, Julian looked over to see Lily Barnes-Shah staring right at him. He couldn't look away. Even from where he stood he could see there was something about the look in her eyes. Something like anger. She looked away first, but that was a feeling he knew all too well.

It was an interesting thing, watching a person make a decision of some gravity. Watching the emotions play out on their face. First uncertainty, followed by a ripple of fear, and then, as their will solidified, and they became certain of their choice, their features would set. Sometimes with determination, other times with confidence, at times even with aloofness.

Watching Lily closely from his place at the bar, Julian saw her push her shoulders back and lift her chin, as if she'd suddenly remembered she was San Franciscan royalty. With no small amount of curiosity he saw her pull away from Lincoln, whose questioning gaze had turned hard.

Julian realised his glass was midway to his lips, as if he'd forgotten what he was doing. He drained the rest of his drink, not tasting any of it, and watched Lily walk away from the two men. He had seen Lincoln's look before. Seen what it could do. It was a symptom of a much bigger disease. A subtle tell that wrote an entire book for Julian about what kind of man Lincoln Harrison was.

He knew he needed more information on what was happening, so he looked to her brother Devan, whose jaw was set. A look of frustration on his face.

Very interesting.

But the two men didn't hold his attention for long. Not when *she* was walking towards him. Not when this beautiful woman, who moved with effortless grace, and who had eclipsed every other being in this room, had her eyes fixed on *him*. It shifted something in his chest. Made every cell in his body come alive. Her presence called to him, and his body was responding without thought.

Julian rested against the bar just as she reached him, leaning his arms on the gold marble. 'I've never seen anyone look more like a lamb to the slaughter,' he said.

A flash of surprise was quickly covered by a polite smile. 'You must not attend enough of these things, then.'

Her voice was lower than he'd expected and he immediately craved hearing it again.

'Julian Ford.' He extended his hand.

She laughed—a delicate, musical sound that crept under his skin—and all he could do was stare.

'I know who you are,' she said, her eyes twinkling. 'And I'm—'

'Lily Barnes-Shah,' Julian responded, looking down at her diamond-shaped face.

The rich warm tones of her skin glowed in the bright light. Her espresso-coloured eyes were bottomless depths…black mirrors that sparkled. They were coloured with a hint of sadness her smile couldn't cover, and there was no discernible point where her irises ended and her pupils began.

Heaven help him if they weren't the most beautiful eyes he'd ever seen.

Lily took his hand in a surprisingly firm grip. A spark unlike anything he had felt before flared at the touch, and a jolt of pure want went right through him. He looked into her eyes and saw surprise and heat there. Julian could only assume it reflected his own.

What the hell was happening to him? No one ever affected him like this, and he was never deprived of female company. He could have anyone he wanted, when he wanted—although admittedly that had occurred with less and less frequency since those interactions had grown tiresome.

He wasn't expecting and wasn't prepared for Lily to jumpstart his need with nothing more than her presence and a handshake.

And he wasn't the only one affected.

He had heard her gasp. Could see the flush now creeping up her skin.

Gently, she pulled her hand away—delicate and

small in his—and as if someone had flipped a switch the people around them seemed to move once again. The hum of voices filled the air. His lungs began working once more, but the atmosphere remained charged. He half expected to see the crackle of electricity zapping between them.

Lily cleared her throat, turning towards the bartender, a pulse fluttering at her neck.

'A Cabernet, please,' she said.

Julian tipped his empty glass, indicating that he wanted a refill, then leaned on his elbow and crossed one foot over the other as he turned towards Lily.

'I wouldn't have expected you to know me,' she said.

'Should I be insulted? You don't know me, and yet you're already making assumptions.'

She let out a soft chuckle. 'I suppose you're right.'

Their drinks were placed on the bar and he watched her lift the red wine to her full lips, his cruel imagination making him think of all the things he'd like to do to those lips.

Get it together! he chastised himself.

'Shall I just assume you know everyone in this room?' she challenged with a cocked brow.

'Yes,' he answered simply.

'I suppose I should expect nothing less from the wunderkind of the Bay Area.'

She took another sip. It was driving him crazy.

Julian's genius had been extensively covered by the media. When you were an industry-leading innovator, with a rags-to-riches story, you were newsworthy material. He had learned to live with it, but hated the idea that one day someone was going to share the entire story of his childhood. The idea made him burn.

'Not just the Bay Area,' he said.

'Wow, you certainly don't have any issues with confidence.'

The teasing smile on her face made him eager for the next one that would appear.

'I see no point in denying the truth. What use do I have for false humility?'

'Is everything black and white with you?'

'I have room for a few shades of grey.'

'But not a rainbow?'

'Definitely not. I'm in technology. I like the simplicity of binary.'

'Maybe there's fun to be had in the complex?' Lily challenged.

Julian took a single step towards her, making her crane her neck to look up at him.

'I agree,' he said, in a darkly sensual voice. 'In taking it apart and reducing it to its simplest parts...understanding what makes it tick.'

Lily shivered under his gaze. She had never been with a man before, but for some reason she was certain Julian would be able to take her apart—which was a wildly inappropriate thought to have about someone she had just met. She had to regain her balance. Take this exchange into safer waters and away from what was pulsing between them.

'From what I hear, taking things apart is what you do best.'

'Then your sources must not hear everything.'

He took a lazy sip of his drink and Lily watched the bob of his Adam's apple as he swallowed.

God, she just could not tear her eyes away from his.

There was no word for the colour of them. Hovering somewhere between green and blue, they reminded her of the most untameable seas. Fierce. Beautiful. Just like the rest of him.

A tiny gold hoop earring twinkled prettily in the helix of his left ear—so out of place with everything else about him. The impeccable suit, the perfect posture, the utter seriousness… It hinted at something hidden. Something she wanted to learn. And it screamed danger. Told her that he wasn't from her world.

She was drawn to him. If she closed her eyes she could still feel the current skittering across her body. The flare of her pulse. Reactions she hadn't ever felt before. Even though they were just bantering, she couldn't control her body's awareness of him. She felt the gruff rumble of his voice when he spoke like a tremor in her world. Lily wanted nothing more than to be around this man all night…

'Are you saying you don't?'

She picked up her wine glass for fear that if her hands were free she might do something terribly reckless. Like touch him again.

'Oh, I do. I will take apart anything that isn't working.'

'Brute.'

Lily thought she almost saw him smile then. Something flashed in his eyes before disappearing entirely.

'Sometimes you need to be.'

He looked away, for a moment, as if deciding whether or not he wanted to say more. Lily held her breath, hoping he would.

'If you had a tree you knew could produce the best fruit but was incapable of it right now, you would tend it. Cut away the rot. Find the source of the problem and eliminate it. Maybe you would have to trim it so far back that it would take a whole seasons for it to recover but once it did, you would have your perfect tree. What use is a business that is bound to fail?' he asked. 'How does that make money? Everyone it supports is in danger of losing their livelihood. It might not be pretty, but sacrifices have to be made—and if that makes me a brute, I'll happily wear the title.'

'Hmm, you care…' She smiled in playful accusation.

'Most would say I'm incapable of it.'

Lily saw the hint of hidden depths in those hard eyes. 'I get the feeling most people don't really know you at all,' she said.

He cocked a perfectly shaped brow. 'That's a bold assumption to make about someone you don't know.'

She jutted out her chin. 'Am I wrong?'

'Not at all,' he conceded.

'You know, you're surprisingly honest…' And after dealing with the machinations of Devan and Lincoln, she found it refreshing.

'Again, should I be insulted?'

'Definitely not. In any case, I don't think I *could* insult you.'

'And why is that?'

'Because to feel insulted you would have to care about what people think, and something tells me you don't.'

'How very astute.'

Having that confirmed shifted something in her. It told her she could trust this man—because if he didn't care what people thought, there was no reason for him to be dishonest or deceptive.

* * *

Julian was enjoying himself with Lily. Her quick, teasing wit and her readiness to go toe to toe with him was a massive turn-on and he was struggling to ignore the attraction.

'Still, everyone is talking about Helios,' Lily said, taking a sip of her wine while keeping her eyes on him.

Julian's last acquisition had been a PR nightmare. The company had had potential, but everything had been wrong with it. He'd had to clean house from bottom to top, and felt no remorse after taking it apart.

'I'm sure they are.'

He glanced over her shoulder to grant himself a small reprieve from her presence, noting that Lincoln had joined another group, but was staring at Lily with anger clear in his eyes.

'Your boyfriend seems to be rather put out that you're talking to me.'

'He's *not* my boyfriend.'

Her tone had a note of finality to it, but there was something else in it that rankled.

'That's a juvenile term anyway.'

The switch from playful to this combination of anger and frustration was jarring. 'I apologise,' he said. 'I assumed you were together.'

'You and everyone else.'

There was a hopelessness to her tone when mere moments before it had been bright and full of life. Something was going on here.

An instinct he'd thought long buried rose to the surface. 'Pick up your drink and follow me.'

She had no reason to do so, having only just met him, but he knew she would. So, without checking to see if she had in fact followed him out, he made his way to the balcony that offered unobstructed views of the spectacular bridge.

He was relieved to find her joining him at the railing. Having Lily out here might get him the answers he wanted, as well as some ammunition. Whatever situation she was in, Julian sensed she hated it, but knew she wouldn't easily reveal what that was. She had no reason to. He had to offer her something to gain her trust enough that she would tell him...

Lily had expected Julian to question her on what he'd witnessed in the ballroom, except he didn't.

'I was once in a situation where everyone thought my life was as good as it got, given where I lived.'

Julian looked out towards the water as he spoke. His tone careful.

'But it wasn't?' she asked.

'Far from it.'

'What did you do?'

Lily wondered if by sheer chance she had found someone who could understand what she was going through. What she needed.

'Everything I could to get myself out.' Julian turned to look at her then. There was something tumultuous in his eyes. 'To live on my terms. To have freedom and peace.'

Lily wanted that too. Desperately.

She didn't know what Julian had seen in her face when he had asked her to step outside with him, but she hadn't expected him to offer this bit of strength to her. A little piece of him, she realised. A kindness...a small offer of himself from a man who gave nothing away.

It made her feel reckless, and before she could stop herself—before she could consider that she had only known him for a few minutes—Lily found herself revealing her situation to this man who made her feel so inexplicably comfortable.

'My father promised me to Lincoln. I'm supposed to marry him. It's what my brother wants,' she said.

Understanding lit his features. 'You're a bargaining chip.'

'Pretty much,' she replied, suddenly realising how impulsive she was being. Wondering if she'd made a mistake telling him.

'And what do *you* want?'

No one had asked her that before. Not one person cared enough but here stood Julian asking how she felt. A lump rose in her throat and she had difficulty talking around it.

'I want the chance to live my life. Whether I end up marrying someone or remaining single for the rest of my life, I want it to be *my* choice. Everyone should get that. Why should I be deprived?'

His unflinching gaze held hers, sending goosebumps up and down her arms.

'You shouldn't.'

He looked away. Immediately she missed the way his eyes felt on her.

Shifting the focus away from herself, Lily asked, 'What do you want from this night?'

She watched him glance though the glass doors at a group of men talking animatedly. A group that included her brother and Lincoln.

'The one thing I can't have.'

She heard the note of frustration in his voice and

understood. She knew exactly how reluctant this community was to let in new money. It was elitist and judgemental.

'I'm afraid they're going to take a lot of persuading.'

'Tell me something I don't know. You should probably go back inside,' Julian said.

'I probably should. They're going to wonder what we've been talking about.'

'Tell Harrison I'm looking to buy a cake,' Julian said, amusement twinkling in his eyes, even though he still did not smile.

Lily choked out a laugh around her wine.

'We'll speak again, sunshine,' he said.

'Julian!' she called, before she disappeared through the doors. 'Your secret is safe with me.'

'Likewise,' he replied.

CHAPTER THREE

WITH A THUNDEROUS RUMBLE, Julian brought his car to a stop in front of a large concrete building with industrial French doors in Fisherman's Wharf. The streets were busy. And there was a cacophony of sounds in the air as he stepped out of his car.

This was not a part of San Francisco he often visited. He had no reason to. He'd moved to this city because it had been the best place to start IRES. The only support he'd had as a young man had been Henry, so the fact that he resided here was a bonus.

Still, he could appreciate the place Lily had chosen for her store.

Lily...

She had been on his mind from the moment he'd set eyes on her. Of course she had been—she was beautiful. However, it was when he'd heard Devan Shah wanted to hand her over to Lincoln Harrison that the cogs of his mind had begun working. It was obvious how entwined those families were, and he knew they could unlock his success in San Francisco and, following that, in the wider US.

Experiencing that intense chemistry with Lily had him forming a plan. One that would greatly benefit him and, if he played it right, save Lily too. He would use her to get closer to Devan. Work on him to secure his support for the deal at Arum and then, once that was in hand, gain the vote of the rest of the board. It was risky, though, as it would spark the ire of Lincoln—the majority shareholder.

There were a few things Julian considered would work in his favour: firstly, Lincoln rarely went against any decision that Devan and the board backed, and secondly, he was more than willing to secure some insurance against Lincoln as a contingency plan. Julian suspected he knew the kind of man he was, so there would be plenty of dirt to find if he looked in the right places. And thirdly, once Julian had insinuated himself into their clique Lincoln would have no choice but to consider IRES. It would look suspicious if he discounted Julian without reason. Especially if he used Lily to garner an invitation into Zenith…

There was also the possibility that with Devan lobbying for Arum to go with IRES none of his back-up plans would be needed.

The first step was to get Lily to agree. Which was why he was outside her shop now.

Pressing the fob in his hand, he locked his black, futuristic sports car, buttoned his grey suit jacket and walked towards glass doors with a quaint sign above it that read *Crème*.

Even for this city full of food, the place was busy.

He opened the door and slipped in quietly. His first thought was how inadequate the word 'bakery' was. Lily's café-patisserie was a kaleidoscope of pastries in every colour fathomable. Every seat was taken, and queues formed at every cake display.

A ribbon of pride wound around his heart. Perhaps it had something to do with how happy she looked here, compared to the sadness he'd seen behind her façade when they had first met. There was something special about her that went further than her brightness and obvious intelligence. Although he didn't quite understand why he felt so strongly, given he had only met her the night before.

An apron with curly writing on it covered her front. Her glossy ebony hair was pulled back into a ponytail that Julian wanted to wrap around his fist. He wondered if she would gasp when he tugged on it. What the skin on her neck would taste like…

He shook away the thoughts. Or tried to. He had been failing at that since last night. He couldn't get her off his mind. From her smile and her eyes to everything she had said, Lily had imprinted herself on his memory.

His urge to pull her into his arms and kiss her wasn't the reason he'd come, but he did like getting a chance to watch her. She handed a box to a customer with a broad smile and greeted the next person. Every face brightened when she spoke.

He couldn't relate.

Being who he was, Julian brought out fear, frowns and clenched jaws. The best he would get were fake smiles.

But Lily wasn't like him. She wasn't made of darkness.

Julian decided to be patient. What he wanted to discuss would need her undivided attention. So he waited and watched.

Lily felt a prickling of awareness. A feeling she hadn't ever experienced until the night before. *He* couldn't be here, though. Why would he be? He knew how little power she had over her family and with the Harrisons. She wouldn't be in the predicament she found herself in otherwise.

Surely she was imagining things.

But one quick glance to the corner of the store told her she wasn't. Julian was in her patisserie, looking sinful and dangerous, with his hands in his pockets and no hint of a smile on his face.

She wondered what it would take to get one out of him. How handsome that would make him. Why didn't he smile? He was certainly capable of humour. She had found that out last night.

When Devan and Lincoln had interrogated her, Lily had actually told them that Julian wanted a cake. She'd had to hide the laugh that had threatened to erupt when their faces had reflected confusion and then suspicion.

She had managed to keep it in until she shut the door of her bedroom later, when breathless laughter had escaped her. Lying in bed, she had found thoughts of Julian spinning wildly. Without even touching her he'd made her *feel*.

When he had stepped into her space it had been as if he had tugged her head back and made her look at him. It had made her achy and flushed. And when he'd walked away after calling her 'sunshine' she'd wanted to beg him to say it again, but she hadn't.

She'd played the sound of his voice over and over in her head until she'd fallen asleep...

She handed a box of pastries over the counter and told one of her assistants that she would be right back.

'Julian,' she said when she reached him. 'This is a surprise.'

'Do you have a moment? We need to talk.'

His eyes were burning into her the same way they had done the night before, making it hard for her to concentrate. The sunlight coming through the glass illuminated half his fair-skinned face while striking the other half in shadow. Her mouth went dry looking at him.

She wanted to touch him. Find out how hard his body was. Run her fingers through the short, soft red hair that was cut so perfectly that even though she expected it to curl over his collar, it never did.

'Um…give me a moment. It's a bit crazy in here. I need to deal with a few more customers then we can talk.'

He gave her a single nod. No words. Just one efficient movement.

She rushed back behind the counter and apologised to her customers before helping them as quickly as possible. In a matter of minutes the queue had cleared, leaving her free to deal with Julian.

'Let's go to my office,' she said.

Her stomach did a little somersault at the thought of being alone with him.

She led him through the passage at the back of the bakery, past the busy kitchen to a closed door at the end. She held it open for Julian, shutting it once he was through and inviting him to take a seat in front of her messy desk. Her computer sat idle to one side. A cork board on the wall was pinned with a slew of slips and papers and different types of ribbon.

To an outsider, it probably looked like chaos. To Lily, it was perfectly ordered.

She took the seat beside his, angling herself towards him. 'What did you want to talk to me about?'

'I need you to listen to me with an open mind. What I'm about to say could benefit us both.'

She was intrigued. But also, given the current state of her life, a little apprehensive. 'I'll try my best.'

'That's all I ask.'

She watched him study her, making her feel even more antsy.

'I have a proposition for you. A mutually beneficial one.'

'Oh…?' She frowned.

His eyes flicked to her forehead before landing on her eyes once again. Lily suspected nothing slipped by his notice.

'I can get rid of your Lincoln Harrison problem. In return, you can help me get close to your brother, and thereby gain access to a group of people that holds a lot of money and influence in this city.'

'What? How?'

Her heart began beating wildly. She was willing to listen to anything that would free her of Lincoln.

'All we have to do is pretend to be engaged.'

That drew her up short.

Lily was certain her heart had now ceased beating. There was certainly no air in her lungs. So she had no idea how she managed to say, 'Engaged…' It somehow managed to sound like a question, a statement and a panicked breath all in one.

'I realise this might seem a bit extreme, but you agreed to try to keep an open mind,' Julian said.

How the hell could he speak so calmly?

She swallowed hard. 'I did.'

'Clearly you are aware of my reputation…' He paused, continuing only once she'd nodded. 'Having you as my fiancée will soften my image. In addition, it will make people more amenable to me joining their circle. Zenith. In terms of your situation, being engaged will make it a lot harder for Lincoln to marry you. You could have your freedom. After an appropriate amount of time we will call the engagement off, by which point you should be out of your brother's house and free to seek any path you wish. I'll make sure you're free. You have my word.'

'Julian…' Lily said on a breath.

She didn't know what to say. How could she trust that Julian would let her go afterwards? She couldn't trust her own family to look out for her. Though she was willing to extend a small amount of trust towards Julian when she told him of the arranged marriage.

'I'll put out the word that we've been seeing each other secretly,' he went on. 'But with your father's sudden passing we realised it was time our relationship was out in the open.'

'I don't know what to say.' She pushed off the chair, pacing to the cork board and back, seeing nothing of her office. 'People already think I'm with Lincoln—or entangled with him in some way. This would be scandalous. And what about the fact that people are genuinely afraid of you?'

'*You* don't ever have to be. I need you to know that. I'll take care of you, Lily. I'm promising you your freedom and I *never* go back on my word.'

She didn't know… This seemed dangerous. Changing an arranged marriage for a fake engagement. Also, Lincoln was vindictive. He wouldn't take kindly to Julian stealing her away.

'The idea is insanity,' she said softly.

Glancing back at Julian, she suddenly felt she could trust that he would protect her. He would be able to handle Lincoln. She was fairly sure of that. This was just such an extreme solution.

She turned around again, closing her eyes. Then she felt his presence at her back. A feeling she wanted to sigh into and a current that made her alert of every little thing around her. The weight of his hands on her shoulders turning her around. The touch searing her right to her depths. There was a flare in his eyes too. The colour darkening, his grip tightening just as her core did. Her breath becoming rapid and shallow. Her body moving closer to his without her realising it....

'You need to get away from him. I can help you.'

Julian's voice had grown hoarse. His head dipped infinitesimally towards her.

'Why do you want to?' she asked.

'Because I've seen the way he looks at you. I've seen it before, and I know that you know what I'm talking about. Is that the life you want for yourself?'

She was right. He *did* notice more than anyone else ever had. She wasn't sure if Devan hadn't seen it, or if he just didn't care enough to protect her from it, but that look on Lincoln's face gave her a horrible feeling about the future.

'I need to get away from him. I just want to live my life...but I'm scared to get stuck in another trap.'

'I know you have no reason to trust me yet, but give me a chance to show you that you can. This will work for both of us. We have the chemistry to make it believable. I know you feel it.'

Lily did. Her body pulsed with the need to close the

tiny gap between them. To run her lips up the strong column of his throat.

'We'll need terms before I consider this any further,' she said, forcing herself to think beyond the lust. 'A definite end point.'

'Agreed. Here's what I propose…'

Julian removed his hands and she wished he hadn't.

Sitting down once more, he gestured for her to do the same, then continued. 'Arum is looking to switch to green energy. I want that deal. A deal with them will open a lot of doors that have been closed to me in San Francisco and the country at large. Once I have it we'll no longer have to see each other, but you'll keep wearing your ring for a while longer. After an appropriate amount of time, you can take it off and move on with your life. You never have to see me again if you don't want to.'

'Ring…?'

'Of course. We'll be engaged.' His lips twitched, as if a smile had fought to be freed but lost the battle. 'We will go on three dates. I will propose to you on the first one. After the third, you will move in with me.'

'Move in? I don't even know where you live!'

Lily panicked. How could she live in the same house as him, as attracted to him as she was, while knowing their every interaction would be fake?

'I live in Sea Cliff. Now you know,' he deadpanned. 'My fiancée can't be living at home with her brother when she should be planning a wedding with me.'

'Valid point…' Lily choked.

'Once this is over you can live anywhere you wish. I will assist you if you require it.'

She had already been looking at apartments, but had

held off on making a decision. She didn't really want to leave Devan alone in that big house when it had been intended to be a home for their family as it grew. Except she also didn't want to stay in a place that reminded her of how badly her family had let her down.

'Lincoln might come after me after we break up.'

'I know men like him, Lily. All we need is time and plenty of public appearances to sell the idea that we're madly in love. Harrison won't want it to seem like he's waited for you. He wouldn't give anyone that kind of power over himself, would he?'

Lily didn't have to think about it. 'No, he wouldn't.'

'I guarantee, before we call it off Lincoln will have someone else on his arm.'

'He would want to seem like he's winning. Probably make some big public announcement,' Lily said, following Julian's thought.

'Precisely. The expectation would shift. When were you meant to have married?'

'Next year.'

'If you agree to this, that will never happen. What do you say?'

This whole idea was madness. Her heart raced just from thinking about it. She would be lying to her brother. Her mother.

But doing so might grant her a life that was all her own. That was what Julian was offering, and all he wanted was a fair shot at a deal that was unfairly being denied to him.

And Julian himself was an attractive part of the package. A fun, thrilling part. Of course this was all fake, but the idea of being around him and getting to know him better—this man who made her feel things she never had—was extremely appealing. Even now, when he was doing nothing more than looking at her, he turned everything inside her molten.

Maybe he could show her the passion she had been denied, even if it was temporary. And maybe…just maybe…she could finally have someone in her corner. Someone she could be honest with and confide in. Heaven knew how much she missed that.

It was hard to trust that everything would work out as he planned, though. It was hard to trust, period. Yet he had resources—power. He could more than adequately take on Lincoln if it came to that. Though she hoped it wouldn't.

If Julian could free her, the least she could do was help him. He was right. This was a mutually beneficial plan, and she could count more pros than cons to this arrangement.

This was insane.

A rash decision.

Don't do anything rash, please. Devan had asked.

Too damn bad!

This was a way out and she would seize it with both hands.

'Let's do it,' she said, surprised by the steadiness of her voice.

A small smirk curved one corner of his mouth and she lost the ability to speak as his face was transformed into something roguish.

'I'll pick you up tomorrow evening. Seven. Wear something you'd like to get photographed in.'

He winked and leaned down to place a quick kiss on her cheek. Sensation exploded throughout her body, but before she could turn her head, maybe kiss him back, Julian had already pulled away, his eyes smouldering.

She saw his jaw flex and then he was striding out of her office…leaving her a nervous, excited, heaving, trembling mess.

CHAPTER FOUR

A DRESS THAT she would like to get photographed in.

Ordinarily an easy decision to make. Not tonight. Lily stood in her large walk-in closet, riffling through rails of beautiful dresses bought off catwalks around the world. None of them seemed right.

There was a lot of pressure on this date and this night. It felt monumental. The first step in taking her life back. Getting out of this pit of desperation and frustration. What dress, if any, would be appropriate?

A part of her that she didn't want to pay attention to wondered if Julian would approve of what she wore. It shouldn't matter. What they had was fake. But when she thought of that kiss in her office, as innocent a touch as it had been, she couldn't deny that she was attracted to him.

For a hairsbreadth of a moment, when she turned her head, she wanted to be kissed by him. Wanted that light brush on her lips.

Lily couldn't remember a time when she wanted that so badly.

It made sense. Julian was, objectively, gorgeous. She couldn't be the only one to respond to him that way.

Yet she hadn't felt so strongly towards anyone else in the past.

Caught in her thoughts, she slipped a dress on.

This is the one, she thought.

The dress she would wear when she announced her relationship with Julian to the world. And her brother.

A flicker of guilt burned in her sternum. She was exposing him, giving Julian access to him, letting him use her to win over Devan and thereby work his way into that elite circle of businessmen.

A voice at the back of mind told her this wasn't what good sisters did.

But what about good brothers?

Did they dangle their sisters in front of predators? No. And so she was left with no choice.

She zipped up the blush-pink dress. Its pleated skirt sat prettily around her knees and the sleeves covered her arms to just below her elbow, warm enough to stave off the mild autumn chill. Lily smoothed her hands over the crystal beaded bands around her waist and admired how the metallic silver threads woven into the fabric caught the light.

It was perfect.

She buckled a pair of strappy, red-soled stiletto sandals on her feet, checked her make-up in the mirror and went downstairs to wait for Julian.

'Are you going out?' Devan asked, the moment she reached the main floor.

'Yes.'

'With whom?'

'I don't see how that's any of your business, Dev.'

Lily walked away but he followed.

'I know it isn't with your friends.'

Lily wanted to laugh. Of course it wasn't. She was twenty-four, but instead of having nights out with people she liked, she avoided them. She couldn't tell them about her arranged marriage. Gossip like that would spread like wildfire. And constantly turning down invitations had seen them drying up altogether. So no, she would not be seeing her friends.

'If you know it's not with them then you already have a good idea of what I'm going to say.'

'Lily…'

Another reprimand. She was growing tired of them.

Heaving a sigh, she spun to look at her brother. 'I'm going on a date, Dev.'

Worry clouded Devan's eyes and then they quickly flashed with anger. 'Is this why you suddenly want out so badly? So you can date someone?'

'I want out because I want my life back. I'm dating someone because I want to.'

'Dating?'

Panic and disbelief warred in his tone. Lily couldn't bring herself to care.

Whatever else Dev was about to say was cut off by the sound of a growling engine. Lily hadn't expected the flare of anticipation in the pit of her stomach that it brought, but there was no denying that she couldn't wait to see Julian.

Julian drove through the tree-lined streets of Presidio Heights. The houses were old and beautiful. The blue and gold sunset sky reflected on their walls and windows. The money that flowed through these streets was clear.

This was where he should have bought a home if he'd

been strategic. It would have placed him in the ideal location to move among the people with whom he was now trying to conduct business. The thought of being here, however, sent an involuntary shudder through him.

His home was the one decision he'd made with his heart, and the freedom he felt every moment he spent in it was worth any trouble now.

After the childhood he had had, being so monstrously trapped in that dark house, now being able to sleep while looking up at the night sky was something he absolutely would never give up.

He let his mind drift to Lily and how trapped she was. Even if she hadn't agreed to this ruse he would have found a way to free her, but she didn't need to know that. No one did. He would teach her how to live for herself, and maybe when she made her own home she would find it to be her sanctuary too.

He turned into the drive of an Edwardian-style mansion and killed the engine of his McLaren Artura. This agreement with Lily was necessary for both of them, and he had zero intention of letting any emotion into the arrangement. Especially after he'd kissed her cheek and burning hot arousal had coursed through him. He had wanted to seize her lips and push her against that ridiculously large cork board. Wanted her to push back against him.

This level of attraction was unexpected, and he had to treat it carefully. He couldn't lose control. There was too much on the line.

He had two goals: help Lily and get the Arum deal. That was what he must focus on.

Getting out of the car, he buttoned his black suit jacket and walked up to the front door, which swung open before he could push the bell. Every thought in his head vanished. There was Lily, with a nervous smile, looking far more beautiful than he could have imagined. The urge to kiss her kicked him so hard he wasn't sure how he didn't choke out a sound.

'Julian!' she greeted him, far too brightly. 'Come in. I just need to fetch my purse.'

He crossed the threshold, losing the battle with himself and leaning down, brushing his lips lightly against her cheek.

'Deep breath,' he whispered in her ear. He heard her exhale, felt pleased that she'd listened. 'Good. Now put your hand in mine.'

His fingers locked around hers as she threaded them together. It was the most peculiar feeling. His heart both sped up and fell at ease all at once.

He closed the door and noticed a suspicious Devan off to one side.

'*This* is who you're dating?'

Irritation burst through Julian. He didn't let it show as he approached. Standing a few inches taller than Devan, he looked down at him and extended his hand. 'Julian Ford.'

'I know who you are.'

'Good, then introductions aren't necessary,' Julian said, keeping his face neutral.

Devan turned his furious gaze on Lily and Julian pulled her closer to him.

'Do you think this is a game, Lily?' Devan asked.

'I assure you it's not,' Julian responded.

'I don't know what you think you're playing at, Ford.'

'I'm not playing at anything, Devan. All I'm doing

is taking my beautiful woman out to dinner,' Julian said evenly.

'*Your* woman? Since when? Last night?' Devan scoffed.

'For months. We kept it quiet because your father assured Lily he would find an agreeable solution to her situation, but since he passed her requests for help have fallen on deaf ears, and things have become somewhat uncertain. That's why I wanted us to stop the secrecy.'

'Is this true, Lily?'

Julian turned to look at her, but she was already staring at him. Paralysing him with those eyes.

'Yes.' She smiled.

'Where did you meet?'

'At the patisserie,' Julian answered without missing a beat, making Lily smile broadly.

'The bakery?'

Julian turned his attention back to Devan. 'I don't think calling it a bakery does it justice, and before you ask, the building next door belongs to a client.' That much was truc.

Julian pressed a kiss to the top of Lily's head and it made her shiver. Something inside him rejoiced at her reaction.

'Why don't you get your purse, Sunshine? We're going to be late.'

She nodded and walked away, directing an uncertain gaze at him as she stepped through the doorway.

'I don't know what game you're playing with my sister, Ford, but I won't tolerate it,' Devan seethed.

'I've already said that I'm not playing games. I don't intend to wait in the shadows while the woman I love is handed over to another man. Lily deserves better than to be treated like that and you know it. Despite what you may think of me, I have no issue with you, Shah, and all I'm here to do is take her to dinner. But just so you know… After tonight, I'm not hiding our relationship. I thought you would appreciate the forewarning.'

Drawing up beside him, Lily announced that she was ready.

'Let's go.' Julian took her hand, leading her out through the front door. He opened the door of his car for her, then rounded the vehicle and slid into his seat.

'A gentleman,' she said with a teasing smile.

The expression on his face was wolfish. One that didn't reach his eyes which were still cold. Predatory. 'Well, I am a man…but I'm certainly not gentle.'

If the words hadn't set her pulse fluttering, the wink surely did it. Lily couldn't help staring at him as they drove off. He looked so at ease. So capable. His white shirt was open at the neck, exposing just a hint of the smooth skin at the base of his throat. Now that she thought about it, every time she had seen him, or a picture of him, he had always been in an impeccably tailored suit. Clean-shaven. Nothing out of place. Not even a strand of hair.

That level of discipline and control was nearly unfathomable. Julian seemed beyond human. It had to be taxing…

Only one thing betrayed that cool, calm exterior—the twinkling earring was the first thing she noticed when she opened the door. It was so at odds with everything else about him and she wondered why—if he'd set his sights on getting into Zenith—he wouldn't just remove it.

'I'm surprised by your choice of car,' she said, breaking the silence.

He frowned. The first real expression she had seen him show.

'Why?'

There was genuine confusion in his tone.

'Given that you're all about renewable energy, I thought you'd be busy trying to save the world.' She grinned.

He let out a rush of air and she wondered if that was almost laughter.

'I'm not the hero of this story, Lily. You'd do well to remember that.' His light eyes flicked to hers, then back to the road. 'And it's a hybrid.'

She let out a peal of laughter that had his lips twitching.

'Thank you for what you did back there,' she said. 'I'm sure Devan is angry, but you were so convincing.'

'I lied to him. I told him I didn't have an issue with him,' he confessed.

'And you do?' Lily wasn't really surprised. After all, her brother was part of the group that had made growth in San Francisco difficult for IRES. 'I guess I can understand that. I am aware of the privilege of my birth. If it wasn't for my surname I wouldn't even be in this group, despite my success. So I want you to know I do get it.'

'That's good to know, but not what I meant. I have an issue with the fact that your brother isn't protecting you from Harrison. I was serious when I said you need to find your own place.'

'I do.' Lily fell silent, staring out of the window.

'Thank you for helping me, even though I'm basically a stranger to you.'

'You're not a stranger. We've been dating for months.'

Lily laughed. There it was again. That hidden humour. It felt so good to be pulled away from her wallowing. She had always possessed the ability to see the positives in any situation—the quintessential eternal optimist—but lately it had become harder to be that person. Especially when she was constantly trying to hide the hurt her family had caused.

'There's something we haven't discussed.' He was all business again. 'As of tonight, we'll be engaged. There will be an expectation for displays of affection.'

'I've thought about that too,' Lily replied. 'It would be weird if we never touched. Give us away... Would you like to set some ground rules?'

'I would.' His eyes softened, as if he was pleased. 'I will only ever touch you if and when you are comfortable with it, and I will only go as far as you want me to.'

'What happens if we need to kiss?'

Julian briefly glanced at her. 'Would you be comfortable with that?'

Lily thought back to his lips on her cheek in her office and how much she'd wanted to meet them with hers.

'Yes, I would.'

She didn't add the *with you* that was on the tip of her tongue. She had never been kissed properly before, never wanted it, so this desire was a little alien, slightly worrying and incredibly thrilling.

'What about you? Is there anything I shouldn't do?' Her cheeks heated. She couldn't believe she was having this conversation with him.

His lips quirked up slightly at one corner. 'No, I'll be fine.'

Of course he would. Unlike her, he wasn't inexperienced. Could he tell that she was?

'Okay, good… Yes. We will hold hands and touch and occasionally kiss. For people to see. Perfect.'

She could tell he was trying not to laugh.

'What?'

'It's going to be fine, Lily.'

She hoped so.

They drove the rest of the way in comfortable silence. Getting engaged publicly was a bold move, and she knew she should be feeling more apprehensive about it, but she wasn't. All she felt was this constant current between her and Julian.

The car came to a stop outside a brick building in the city. One of the many warehouses that had been converted into modern masterpieces. Julian pressed a warm hand between her shoulder blades, guiding her inside. She had to fight the tremor his touch unleashed.

'I can't believe you got a table here,' Lily said as they stepped through the glass doors.

'There's nothing I can't do.'

'Don't look now, but I think your humility is showing,' she teased.

The corner of his eyes crinkled, but still he didn't smile.

The waiting list for this Michelin star restaurant was months long, so she couldn't really blame him for being cocky. And, as amazing as the food was, it was also a place to be seen. No doubt there would already be pictures of the two of them entering together. And the fact that Lily could feel the heat from Julian's body as they moved told her exactly what those pictures would look like.

'Mr Ford,' a hostess in black greeted him. 'Your table is right this way.'

A small gasp left her when Julian took her hand in his, and a pleasurable tingle travelled all the way up her arm. She plastered a smile in place and walked alongside him as they were led up a flight of floating stairs and past a sea of tables. There wasn't an empty seat on either floor, and she could feel the burn of all the eyes on them.

'Your table,' the hostess announced, standing next to a table for two out on the small balcony.

They would be in perfect view of everyone inside, yet their conversation would remain private.

Julian pulled out a chair and kissed her cheek once she was settled, then rounded the table to his own seat. His eyes were intense.

There was a small soft smile on the hostess's face as she handed them their menus, then left.

The pull he had on her was so strong Lily had to repeat *fake engagement* in her mind until she could smile and speak without her words sounding like a plea for him to kiss her.

She picked up her menu for a distraction, but the words made very little sense. Thankfully Julian didn't force her to make conversation. At least not yet. But when his leg brushed against hers under the table her body stiffened. Finally, a waiter appeared and she heard Julian order, saying words she was grateful for because they would take her mind off all the ways her body was reacting.

'I'll have the poached lobster and a club soda with lime.'

'The same for me, please,' she said.

Julian could have ordered cardboard and she would have said that she'd have the same. She forced her scattered thoughts into some semblance of order, because if she was going to spend any amount of time with this man she couldn't let their chemistry derail her.

'Can I ask you a question?' she said.

'Of course.'

'Do you not drink alcohol?'

'No.'

'At all?'

She was curious now. She remembered the globe bar in her father's office. The brandy he and Arthur Harrison would sip during their long discussions. The golden liquid flowing whenever they entertained. It had almost seemed like a bonding ritual. If Julian didn't join in with that, he was setting himself apart from these people in yet another way.

'At all.'

'Why?'

She saw his jaw flex, a flash of anger in his eyes, but when he spoke his voice was even and smooth, as always.

'I grew up with an alcoholic. I've seen what alcohol does. There's no room for that in my life, and while you are with me you will remember that.'

That hard tone only made her want to know more. What had happened to him?

'I will. I promise. Can I ask who it was?'

'My stepfather.'

It seemed that was all he was going say so she didn't pry. 'I'm sorry you had to deal with that.'

She grew quiet, trying to put a picture of Julian together, but he was a highly complex puzzle and she only had a few pieces so far.

'Just ask me what's on your mind.' He smirked. 'I can see those cogs turning.'

She let out an embarrassed chuckle at having been caught, but she wasn't going to squander the chance to collect more information.

'Okay… You seem to have come up with this idea rather quickly, and I'm just wondering how you were able to. I mean, being my fiancé makes it impossible for you to have a partner.'

'That's easy. I don't have one.'

'How is that possible?' she blurted.

Julian leaned forward, elbows folded on the table. 'I'm glad you think I'm so desirable.'

'I just meant—'

'The answer is simple, Lily. I don't do relationships.'

That seemed ridiculous. The man was smart, sexy, and so far seemed like a good enough person.

'Why?'

'Why do you want to know?' He smirked again, but this time there was no humour in his expression. 'Think you'll be the one to fix me? I'm a grown man. I don't need to offer reasons for my behaviour.'

He was right. He was free to do what he wanted. It just seemed wrong.

'You don't. And I don't think that. One, I may not know you very well, but I don't think there's anything to fix. Two, I'm trying to get to know you since we will be engaged. And three, I'm very aware of what this is, Julian, but we don't have to be strictly business partners—we can also be friends.'

'I don't have those either,' he stated simply.

Didn't that sound lonely?

'Okay, so what do you do for fun?'

'I work. I tinker.'

Lily thought about Crème and all the time she spent there. All the late nights perfecting recipes alone. She loved that time, so she really couldn't say much to him because hadn't she become the same way?

'Ah, yes, the genius.' She grinned. 'It's funny, you don't *look* like a genius.'

Why was she trying to provoke this obviously tightly wound man?

'Why? Because you buy the media's narrow-minded depiction of what intelligence looks like?'

'Of course not!'

Yet that was exactly what she was thinking—purely because the idea of Julian as a shy, socially awkward person was highly entertaining.

His eyes twinkled in that way they did whenever they flashed the smile the rest of his face wouldn't allow. 'It's both good to know and a little concerning that you're such a bad liar.'

'That's a compliment, Julian. No one should be good at lying. Are *you*?'

'You have no idea…'

But she did. She'd heard him telling her brother he loved her. It was the first time a man had ever said he loved her, and it was a lie. A necessary one, but it left an awful taste in her mouth. And that was her problem, not his.

She pushed on with her questions, only pausing when their food was served before asking, 'How old are you?'

'I thought you'd heard all about me?' He cocked a brow and it was maddening.

'I don't keep a dossier on you.' She rolled her eyes.

He gave a chuckle! Finally! It seemed to surprise them both.

'Thirty.'

As their dinner progressed, Lily found she was able to interpret Julian's subtle tells. When he was amused, when he didn't want to answer a question, when something deeper stirred in him but he wouldn't let it see the light. And, as much as she hadn't expected it, she found she was truly enjoying herself. Talking to Julian was easy, and he made her feel lighter, unburdened in a way that she hadn't experienced in a long time. He drew laughter from her easily. Made her smile.

She watched him move their two glasses aside and reach over to take her hand in his.

'Are you ready for this?' he asked.

'Yes.' She was calmer than when he had collected her, comfortable now that she had got to know him just a little bit. Her life waited on the other side of this decision and she was ready to live it.

He kept his eyes on hers, stroking his thumb back and forth across her knuckles, spreading a white-hot heat that pooled in her core. She watched him slip a hand into his coat pocket and withdraw a black velvet box that he placed between them, pulling his hand away from hers to open the lid with a click.

And even though Lily knew this wasn't real, and she knew Julian didn't love her, she couldn't breathe. Couldn't reach into the box and pluck that amazing ring out. And it was amazing. Timeless. Something she would have chosen for herself. A large princess cut diamond in a platinum band set with a series of pavé diamonds.

'Lily, marry me.'

It wasn't a question…wasn't a request. It was a statement convincing her that she could place her trust in him. Telling her that they were in this madness together.

'Yes,' she choked, surprising herself at how easily the word fell out.

She'd worried that it would be hard to say yes when the time came, but it wasn't. For whatever reason, her *'yes'* felt right.

Julian pinched the ring out of the box and slid it onto her finger then brushed his lips across her knuckles. The world disappeared.

'I'm going to kiss you now,' he said softly, his eyes on hers, and when she nodded with a whispered 'Okay', he pulled her to her feet and stepped up to her until their bodies were almost touching. Until she had to crane her neck to look up at him. At the hunger in his eyes.

Lily had always avoided kissing Lincoln, and had thought she must be wired differently because she hated the idea of it. It was why she had turned away so his lips never met hers. Why she'd felt less than nothing.

But now…

Now her heart raced and her body pulsed. Now she could hear nothing but thunder in her ears. Now all she could do was drown in those darkened eyes, crave the heat of his body.

Julian grasped her chin between his thumb and forefinger, controlling her with ease as his lips lowered to hers. Brushing softly, gently. Once…twice. And then his tongue followed, tasting her.

She mewled, felt her legs growing weak, but a strong arm wrapped around her waist, fusing her to his hard body, and she gasped, allowing him to slide his tongue into her mouth, coaxing hers to dance with him.

And it did. Nervously at first, but then Julian growled deeply at the back of his throat, and it was the single most erotic sound she had ever heard. It made her confidence swell. Allowed her to take his bottom lip between hers, to press her hands against the hard muscle of his stomach, push them up until they landed on his chest, his white shirt bunched in her fingers.

And still he kissed her. Dominated her mouth. His lips slid with urgency now. They were lost. Lost to this stormy tempest of a kiss that kept sucking them into its depths only to crash into each other again and again.

His taste and his smell, like rich leather and spice and a hint of coffee, submerged her. She thought she could kiss him for ever. But the sound of clapping broke the spell and Julian wrenched away from her lips, his chest rising and falling as if he had run miles. His eyes were dark.

Lily hadn't known what to expect in kissing Julian, but she couldn't have imagined it would be like this. Kissing him had been life-altering. And she wanted to do it again.

CHAPTER FIVE

JULIAN'S JAW WAS clenched so hard his teeth were in jeopardy of shattering. He held the steering wheel in a death grip. There was no air in the car. Only a tension so thick it was almost physically suffocating.

Lily wasn't looking at him. Her eyes were set firmly on the road ahead. Dainty hands neatly clasped in her lap. Still. So very still.

Despite this, every minute shift in her body set off a gong in his head. Julian half expected to see something physical, tethering them together. But there was just the invisible magnetism between them that had ratcheted up to alarming levels. He had never been so aware of a woman's body before.

It was all the fault of that kiss.

They'd had chemistry before, and now that they'd lifted the lid on it, it was like opening Pandora's box. Unleashing a power between them that they hadn't seen coming. One that had led to this tension…all the easy conversation from before obliterated.

Julian wanted to call out to Lily. Make sure she was okay. That would have been the right thing to do. But he couldn't. It would mean unclenching his jaw, and that pain gave him back his control and the ability to think straight, which was exactly what he needed now. He had to master himself, because if he didn't his mind immediately went back to the kiss.

He'd had to kiss her. People had needed to see. That was the whole reason he had chosen that restaurant in the first place. No doubt pictures of his proposal would already be flying around San Francisco at speeds that would seem incomprehensible.

So he'd slipped the ring on her finger and then had to kiss her—because what man would not do so after getting his *yes*? He'd been prepared for that. He'd thought it would be a simple kiss. But, Christ, he'd been wrong!

The moment their lips had touched something in him had bowed to Lily. As if he had been searching for an answer his whole life and here she was, giving it to him. He hadn't been ready for the surge of arousal, for her less than confident response.

Julian had kissed many women in his life, so the inexperience of her touch had been immediately noticeable to him, telling him he had to be gentle. But he hadn't wanted to be, and when she'd found the confidence to kiss him back he *really* had not wanted to be gentle. He'd wanted to swipe the table clear and pin her down on it, kissing her until her lips were bruised from the force of his want. And even though he'd had to hold back, he'd still drowned in her.

He could still feel the sweet touch of her hands on his chest. His eyes flicked down to his shirt. Deep creases wrinkled the fabric where her hands had fisted it. She'd wanted more of him and he had wanted to give it to her. If that clapping hadn't returned his senses to him Julian shuddered to think where they might have ended up.

Lily could make him lose control. Therefore Lily

was a danger to him. To his goals. He had remained focussed on IRES for years. It was the only good thing in his life. He needed to make sure his company thrived, because the success of his company was what made him worth something. More than that, the greater the success of IRES, the further away from the poverty of his childhood he moved. But, despite all that, he still wanted to kiss her again.

It was not acceptable.

He had worked too damn hard to get where he was just to lose sight of what mattered because of some attraction. He hadn't walked out of his stepfather's house, never to return, only to fall down now, before he could have everything he wanted.

He had been through too much, sacrificed too much, to let his wayward libido screw everything up. Emotions…raging attraction—they all clouded the mind. After all his mother had been through Julian didn't want that. He needed Lily and she needed him for a purpose. If they blurred the lines it would help neither of them.

He couldn't let a kiss like that happen again. For both their sakes.

Now, his biggest concern was to get her comfortable with him again—because if she stayed this tense around him no one was going to believe they were engaged. Devan was suspicious enough already, and he needed the man to see how happy Lily was with him. It would get him on Julian's side for the Arum deal, and soon enough Julian would leverage this 'relationship' to secure other contracts.

All of it would start with Lily relaxing. The problem was it wasn't in Julian's nature to apologise—and he didn't want to apologise for that kiss.

'Lily…'

Her body stiffened, but slowly she turned towards him, her gaze averted. 'You don't have to say anything.'

He had only seen her confidence. The insecurity written in her posture now didn't sit right with him.

'I'm sorry,' she said.

Julian was taken aback. What on earth did she have to be sorry for?

'For what?'

'The kiss.'

Julian swung the steering wheel, pulling over under a large tree. He turned in his seat, studying her intently. 'What are you talking about?'

'I—I got carried away, and then I saw the look on your face…'

'Lily, look at me.' When she didn't, he held her chin and forced her to. 'You have *nothing* to apologise for. We're consenting adults, we kissed, and it was good. Clearly there is something here—and if there was anything written on my face it was frustration that I wanted you like that in public.'

She tried to look away, but he wouldn't let her.

'Would it help you to know that I want to kiss you again right now? Except that isn't what this is…so I won't.'

Julian could see doubt in her eyes as to whether she should believe his words.

'No one is going to believe you're happily engaged to me if you're this tense,' he told her. 'Is that what you want?'

'No,' she responded softly.

'You need to be as comfortable with me as you were

before.' He had enjoyed that. Not something he wanted to dwell on right now. 'Give me your hand.'

'What?' She frowned.

'Give me your hand,' he repeated.

He waited patiently for her to place her hand in his. Once she did, he held the back of it and placed it on his chest, guiding her hand up and along his shoulder, under his jacket, ignoring the way it seared through him. He took her touch up to the side of his neck, watching the way her breathing had become even and the tension in her body had given way to fascination.

'I am just a man…' He let go of her hand, felt her skim it over his cheek, slightly rough from the day's growth. 'You're wearing my ring. You can touch me without apology, Lily.'

Because he liked it. He liked it so much he wanted her to keep touching him.

'All we have to do is just keep in mind what we're doing here. What we're both trying to achieve.'

Lily nodded, pulling her hand away.

Julian walked Lily to the front door with his hand pressed to her back. Devan's car was in the driveway, and he wondered if her brother would be watching to find some tell that this was all a ruse. He wanted to tell Lily to touch him, but he didn't need to. As if she could read his mind, she wrapped her arms around his neck, hugging him fiercely.

His own arms automatically came around her in response. He was learning how she felt against him. How small her waist was…how easily he engulfed her.

'Remember we're engaged now. If you need anyone, you call me first,' he instructed her.

Then, because the temptation was too great, he kissed her cheek. And when she let go of him he placed another on her lips.

'Goodnight, Julian.' She smiled broadly, then stepped into the house.

He climbed back into his car, ignoring all the things Lily made him feel. It was obviously a side effect of the near celibate life he had been living lately. It was catching up with him now. That was the only explanation.

He refused to dwell on how beautiful Lily had looked on that balcony. How her smile had made him feel, And as he approached his home he put all thought of her aside. Stepping into the modern house set into the cliff, with all its windows offering him unmatched views of the bay, Julian felt the familiar sense of peace that came from being here…alone.

He placed his phone down on the entrance table, and saw a message from Henry flash on the screen.

What are you doing? Lily Shah?!

Julian called his mentor.

'Are you out of your mind?' came Henry's voice, which was coloured with concern. 'The Shahs and the Harrisons are so intertwined everyone knows she's meant to end up with Lincoln.'

'Does everyone know or just expect it?' Julian asked. 'Because what I know is that *I'm* the one in a relationship with her and it's me that she's engaged to.'

Julian walked onto the terrace, felt the chill night breeze ruffling his hair.

'Is Lincoln Harrison really someone you want to

anger? Christ, Julian, you want the Arum deal. How is pissing him off going to help?'

Julian thought back to the way Lily had tensed when Lincoln had touched her. How he'd looked at her… He felt his stomach roil as buried memories surfaced to torment him, as if living through it hadn't been enough. The familiar burn of rage rolled through him.

'Don't worry, Henry, I know what I'm doing.'

'Do you? Why now?'

'Yes, I do. And it's because her father's dead. I'm just letting the world know she's taken. That she has been for a while. Why do you think this has been such a secret? I know what the expectations were.'

'That still leaves Harrison. He's the one who could veto IRES getting the energy deal, even if you have Shah on your side.'

'I'm aware of that.'

Julian was also aware of the fact that Lincoln did not often go against a decision when he would be the only opposing vote, and if his plan to get Devan and the board on his side worked, then Lincoln wouldn't risk the scrutiny of his society peers.

'So what is this? Have you found someone you could love more than your company?'

Henry's question was ridiculous. Love would never be a consideration. Everything Julian was doing was for IRES. But that didn't mean it had to benefit only him.

From the moment he'd seen Lily he had felt a protective instinct unearth itself. He had failed his mother, but he was powerful now, and this time would be different.

'They're completely different. In any case it doesn't matter, because this whole damn city will know she's with me.'

'I hope you know what you're doing.'

Henry hung up, leaving Julian to stare at the phone in his hands. From the moment he'd stepped into Crème Lily had been under his protection. That was no lie. He wouldn't leave her to deal with people like Lincoln Harrison. The man had him thinking of his stepfather, in a crumpled heap on the floor, with Julian standing above him feeling pure satisfaction.

Which was exactly why he couldn't allow himself to get emotionally invested. It wasn't part of the deal, and at the end of the day the only thing he needed to keep sight of was where he was going to take IRES once these people accepted him.

CHAPTER SIX

LILY SAT IN her office, attempting to work. Her door was shut and she had asked not to be bothered while she dealt with everything that required her attention. Except only one thing had it...and it sparkled on her finger.

She couldn't stop thinking about their date. Sure, it hadn't been real, but she had genuinely enjoyed Julian's company.

She toyed with the ring. When he had said she would be wearing one she'd never imagined it would be something quite so beautiful. Something that suited her so perfectly. Of course Julian couldn't have known that.

Julian...

When she closed her eyes she could still feel his lips on hers. That kiss had made her forget where she was, who she was. Just thinking about it had her breath coming in pants. Just as his had done.

She'd been so convinced she had ruined everything by getting carried away. They'd just needed people to see them being affectionate. Acting. That was what he'd been doing. But no one could be that good an actor, could they?

No, the kiss had been real. He'd said he wanted to kiss her again, and she should be grateful that they had such intense chemistry. It would work in their favour. Even Devan had bought the act.

He had been waiting for her arrival home, and all he had said was, 'So it's real?'

When she had nodded, he'd left her standing in the hall. That was the last time she had seen him, but she hoped that his reaction was a sign their plan was already working.

Her mind was firmly focussed on a man who held the weight of the world in his sea-coloured eyes. She sensed that there was so much more to him that he was likely hiding behind thick, high walls. But why? He seemed so hard, but never cold. So controlled, never smiling, and yet his eyes often lit up with humour.

And in the car he had been kind. Reassured her. Made her comfortable. Yet he'd also warned her that he wasn't a hero. Something told her he really did believe that. In fact, there had been several warnings and they all said the same thing: *Don't get attached.*

There was no risk of that. Lily wouldn't let herself forget what was at stake. Her freedom. Her happiness.

That was a feeling she hadn't had much of recently. She was still mourning her father, but instead of getting a chance to work through it, she was having to deal with the anger she harboured at him not fulfilling his promise. The abandonment she was trying to convince herself didn't exist after her mother had left her to deal with her own grief and decided not to be around to help her children. The frustration of only having her brother to turn to now, when he didn't care.

That was why this plan with Julian had to work.

She would be getting just as much out of this as he would. Maybe she wasn't after a deal worth millions, but some things were worth more than money. If only her family would realise that.

It was at that moment that her phone rang. Lily snatched it off her desk, sneaking a quick glance at the name on the screen before answering.

'Hi, Mom.'

Lily's heart raced in her chest. She knew her mother would most likely be disappointed in her, but she reminded herself that her family had broken her trust, so she had nothing to apologise for.

'Lily, is it true? You're engaged?'

It was the first conversation they had had in weeks, and the first words her mother said weren't full of concern for her daughter who had recently lost her father but rather about her engagement. It broke Lily's heart, but she refused to let the hurt show.

'It's true,' Lily said, injecting as much excitement as she could into her voice.

'To Julian Ford? I didn't even know you knew him! What about Lincoln? You're meant to marry *him*.'

Lily could almost see the frown on her mother's face.

'Yes, to Julian. I was never going to marry Lincoln, Mom. Julian and I have been together for a while.'

'So why haven't I heard about this? Or met him?'

'Because we had to keep it a secret while the Lincoln situation was supposed to be dealt with, but I couldn't wait any longer. I want Julian. I'm his.'

'Lily…' her mother said sternly.

It wasn't a tone she'd heard from her very often. Not when she and her mother had been close. But all that was lost now.

'Your father went to a great deal of trouble to secure your marriage to Lincoln. He knew what was best and now that he's gone—' her mother's voice broke on the word '—you should honour his wishes.'

'No,' Lily replied.

'Lincoln can secure your future, and your brother's future. What can Julian Ford offer you? Think of your family.'

'Lincoln means nothing to my future. This is about Arum. Julian can give me everything I want.'

That was true. He was helping her take her life back. Putting her in control of her destiny.

'Why can't you be happy for me?' Lily finished softly.

'You have never mentioned this man before. The Harrisons are like family...'

Lily wanted to point out that she could never have spoken to her mother about Julian when all she'd wanted was blind obedience to her father. She bit back the words only because she knew her mother was blinded by grief and wanted them all to hold on to every part of Sam Shah.

'You don't know Lincoln like I do,' Lily said evenly.

'I can't support this engagement, Lily. You belong with Lincoln. Honour your father.'

What about me? she almost asked.

'Then don't support it. None of you care about me anyway. Julian makes me happy and I'm going to be with him.'

Lily hung up on her mother. It took every bit of strength in her to do so.

She stared at the phone, willing herself not to cry. She couldn't trust her family to be on her side. To protect her or support her.

It didn't matter. She and Julian had a plan.

Lily took another look at her ring. 'I'm engaged,' she whispered to herself. 'What would a newly engaged woman do?'

The answer, she realised, was celebrate. She would show off her ring to her friends and family. Tell the world how happy she was. Well, she had no friends to speak of now, her family weren't happy, and posting all over social media would be unfitting for someone of her station. Which was fine. Because there was really only one person she wanted to see. The one in all this with her.

Deciding it would look good for them both, Lily locked her office behind her and made her way to the front of the shop, where she put together a box of pastries. Leaving one of her assistants in charge, she climbed into her car and drove to the financial district.

Though she had never been there before, she knew exactly where the IRES building was located. A tall glass and steel structure, it was the closest of them all to the pier. As she drove around it to park in one of the guest bays Lily saw at the entrance a large wireframe sculpture of the earth surrounded by a solid green circle with two leaves on top.

She made her way to the reception desk and was shown up to the top floor without having to say who she was. Realising that Julian had obviously cleared her to enter the building made her smile. He'd thought of everything, which was reassuring.

An immaculately dressed brunette greeted her as soon as she got out of the lift.

'Good morning, Miss Shah. Please follow me.'

Lily wasn't sure what she'd expected the inside of Julian's building to look like but, examining the white walls and floors with light grey furnishings and pops of green throughout the space, she figured she should have expected something like this. The no-nonsense décor seemed on point for him, but there was still a welcoming quality to the space. And the most impressive thing was that it didn't interfere with the spectacular view outside.

'Mr Ford, your fiancée is here to see you,' the brunette announced, holding open the door to a massive corner office.

Julian flicked his gaze up from his laptop and Lily was lost in the force of it.

'Thank you,' he said to his assistant. 'Hold my calls.'

Lily didn't hear the door close. She was too focussed on Julian's body as he rose from the chair and stepped around a large, frosted glass desk. He was in a dark blue suit today. Butterflies took flight in her stomach. An overwhelming urge to touch him seized her.

'Hi…' she breathed, then cleared her throat and tried again. 'Hello, Julian.'

His eyes flashed as he stopped in front of her. His thumb pulled her bottom lip free from her teeth. 'Is everything okay?'

'Yes, I just thought it might be nice if I brought my fiancé something from the bakery.'

She held the box out to him, and he took it with the utmost care. He leaned down to kiss her on her cheek. Her skin burned.

'Thank you.'

Lily kept her eyes on him as he lifted the lid on the box, his eyes crinkling with amusement as he set it down on the table.

'I thought I'd bring something for your employ-

ees…you know, because their boss is such a brute.'
She grinned.

His arms came around her waist and she watched,
spellbound, as a broad, beaming smile broke through.

She'd thought Julian would be handsome with a
smile on his face. That was like thinking Michelangelo's
David was a nice sculpture. A criminal understatement.

He was devastating. Deep dimples popping. Perfect
white teeth gleaming. His eyes shining so bright. His
face was transformed. Resplendent. It was like the sun
coming out on cloudy day.

His smile was breathtaking…why did he hide it
away? What had happened to him?

Lily resolved right then to bring a smile to his face
as often as she could.

But she was already attracted to him…if he smiled
like this often she would be in serious trouble.

'Need sweetening, do I?'

She wrapped her arms around his neck, still thrown
by her reaction to him. 'Maybe…'

'Cinnamon rolls aren't very French,' Julian teased.

His usually low, smooth voice was somehow richer
with the smile colouring it. As if he was one step away
from laughter.

'No, they're not,' she replied, thinking that no doubt
people on the other side of his glass-walled office would
be watching. 'But the exclusion of them from any bakery is sacrilegious.'

'That's a strong opinion to hold on a bun.'

'And the only acceptable one.'

Lily barely paid attention to her words because her
entire body screamed at her to kiss him. That once
wasn't enough. She knew she had to marshal some con-

trol over herself before they fell into another embrace like the night before—except it would be far less appropriate in his office.

'Have you seen the news?' he asked.

When Lily shook her head, he unhooked her arms from around his neck, giving her engagement ring a quick kiss that had her melting before handing his tablet to her.

'I've been at the bakery since four this morning,' she said. 'But my mother did call me about it.'

'How did that go?'

'Not great,' she admitted.

There were several tabs open on his tablet, all with news of their engagement. Some of the media sites ran with pictures that had obviously been taken by other patrons at the restaurant, while others simply had individual pictures of them side by side.

'I had my PR people issue a release last night. Now our story is the only one everyone knows.'

'Perfect. Thank you, Julian.' She locked the device and handed it back to him.

He placed it on the table and leaned against the edge. 'Did Devan say anything?' he asked.

Lily shook her head walking towards the floor-to-ceiling window. She could see so much from here. The Ferry Building sprawled below her feet. The Bay Bridge stretching out to the horizon. The water glittering as if diamonds floated on its surface.

Her heart beat a staccato pulse as Julian's heat eclipsed her back. She told him of her interaction with her brother and he agreed that it had been better than anticipated.

'I had another reason for coming here,' Lily said, turning to face him.

'What's that?'

'I would like to plan our second date.'

Julian was struggling to keep his hands to himself. From the moment Lily had walked in all he'd wanted to do was hold her again. Kiss her like he had done on that balcony. The kiss on her engagement ring had been a slip of control that frustrated him, but he'd be lying if he said it hadn't excited him at the same time.

She had her hair tied up and a cobalt top over jeans, and Julian thought he had never seen a more beautiful woman. He could no longer recall the face of anyone who might have come before, and he didn't understand what it was about her in particular that made his blood sing.

'You would, would you?' he asked.

'Yes, all you'd have to do is be at Crème tomorrow evening. Eight.'

'The point is for people to see us,' he replied, even though the idea of being alone with Lily was rather enticing. Especially since he hadn't got much sleep the night before, because every time he'd closed his eyes he could feel the pillowy softness of her lips, or her hands on his neck, or the way she'd looked when she'd opened the front door...

'They will. I'll be closing up at five. Everyone will be gone by six. And when your car is parked for hours in front of my *closed* store word will spread.'

'Fine, I'll be there.'

'Great. Well, I have work to get back to.'

'I'll walk you out.'

He took Lily's hand, letting his office door swing shut behind him. It was like trying to hold on to the lightning crackling between them. The air became so heavily charged he was certain everyone on the floor could feel it. Certainly the craned necks as they passed people indicated as much.

He took Lily to a secondary bank of elevators. They had a lot less traffic. He didn't quite comprehend why he did this. After all, people needed to see them together. And yet he wanted a moment with her that wasn't on show…

He pressed the button to go down and the doors slid open instantly. He let her enter first, then pressed the button for the ground floor. Smoothly the doors slid shut, and with every moment that passed Julian's willpower slipped just that little bit more, until her nearness and her scent and the current running between them made it snap altogether.

He punched the red button on the panel, bringing the elevator to a jerking halt, and crashed his lips down upon Lily's, slamming her back against the black mirrored wall. There wasn't even the tiniest hint of hesitation from her as she kissed him back, her hands coming up to cradle his face. Their lips slid together as his body pressed up against hers, and a tidal wave of arousal crashed through Julian, burning him up from the inside out.

His hands slid down her body and she whimpered, the sound slicing through him. He grasped her wrists, pinning them above her head in one of his large hands, with the other pulling her thigh up around his hips, letting his arousal grind against her. A moan fell from her mouth and he growled. Beastly. Hungry. He kissed a path to her jaw, down her neck. His tongue tasted the sweetness of her skin. The scent of her flowery perfume and vanilla was on every inch of her.

'Julian…' she breathed against his ear. 'We can't do this here.'

Here?

In a lift. In his office.

He let his forehead fall to the crook of her neck, taking a breath. He eased her leg down, but his breathing still hadn't returned to normal.

'It might be a bit inappropriate to make out with the boss at his office,' she said.

He appreciated her trying to get them back on solid ground, but he could see the glazed look in her eyes, just the same as his.

He pulled himself up to his full height and dropped a kiss on her forehead. 'There's nothing inappropriate about me kissing my fiancée.'

He pressed the button once more and the elevator continued its descent. He walked her to her car and watched her drive away, cursing the way she threatened his perfectly ordered world.

CHAPTER SEVEN

HEADS TURNED AS a loud roar echoed through the streets of Fisherman's Wharf. Julian brought the car to a stop outside Crème but didn't immediately get out. Instead, he stayed where he was and looked through the large windows at the dimly lit store. He was dreading this date.

He had been irritated with himself since the incident in the elevator. Lily was challenging his control, and that wasn't something he could tolerate— because who would he become without it?

Images of his stepfather flashed through his mind. The man's violence. His own. Julian couldn't let his control be challenged because he refused to turn into the kind of man that his mother had loved despite all he had done to her. Refused to be the kind of person to fall in love.

The leather on the steering wheel complained at his wringing grip.

He had to reinforce his walls because he knew Lily had the potential to pass through those barriers. He didn't invite love or affection into his life. They were temporary. Inevitably ripped away by circumstance or time, leaving you battered and broken. Julian couldn't afford that. He had to guard himself against her.

Their touches in the office had been for show, calculated for the most part, so kissing her fingers, wanting for his own moment with her in the elevator—all that had to stop.

Julian got out of the car, shut the door and walked into Crème. The lights were low. A candle burned on one table that was perfectly set with shiny cutlery and tall glasses.

The table, while not directly in front of the window, was within perfect view of the street. Perfect to sell the idea of an intimate dinner with a bit of privacy. No doubt there would be pictures taken through the window.

Julian felt Lily enter before he saw her. He had to stave off annoyance with himself as he turned around. She wore a flowing red dress that tied around her neck. Her hair was loose, falling in a straight, silky sheath down her back. Diamonds sparkled in her earlobes. The punch of her beauty knocked the air from his lungs.

'Hi, Julian.'

She smiled, kissing him lightly on the cheek. He thought the kiss was far too fleeting—which was ridiculous, given that he had decided to keep his walls up around her.

'Have a seat. I'll be right back.'

She was gone before he had a chance to respond.

He took his seat and waited for Lily to return. This space felt too intimate. He should have insisted on planning this date. Then they would be elsewhere. Somewhere more public.

Lily returned with two large white bowls. The aroma emanating from them was heavenly.

'Here you go,' she said brightly, setting one bowl in front of him before placing the other on the table and taking her seat.

'You made this?'

Of course she had. Julian had thoroughly researched her before he'd ever set foot in Crème.

'I did. I know boeuf bourguignon isn't the fanciest French dish I could have prepared, but it's just so good.'

She reached for a carafe filled with chilled iced tea, but he beat her to it, pouring the cold reddish gold drink into their glasses, then setting it aside.

He picked up his cutlery and hesitated. She'd cooked for him. It shouldn't mean anything. It didn't, he told himself. So what if the last time a woman had prepared him a meal he'd been fourteen and dressed in thrift store clothes? It wasn't a big deal.

But as he looked into his bowl his mind was taken to a small table under a fluorescent light, with a nervous, scared, happy woman who shared his eyes. The person he'd loved the most and hadn't been able to save.

'Is everything okay?' Lily asked from across the table, watching him carefully.

'Fine.' He took a sip of his drink, bringing life back to his parched mouth, and then set about eating this meal that was definitely not making him feel anything. 'This is good. You're very skilled.'

'Was there ever any doubt? Did you not have one of my cinnamon rolls?'

He could see that she fully expected him to say no, but what fun would that be? She had him off balance tonight. It was time he returned the favour.

'I did.'

'You did?'

'Yes. All of them.' He smirked.

'A-all of them? I didn't expect… I didn't think you had much of a sweet tooth.'

'I don't, but as my fiancée personally delivered them to me the least I could do was eat them.'

Lily laughed. Not politely, the way someone would expect of her, but a deep belly laugh. 'Just when I think I have you figured out…'

'You shouldn't think that. Ever.'

No one ever got close enough to him to do so, and no one ever would. He dictated who entered and left his life, and he was quite happy for the only person who stayed in it to be Henry. As attracted to Lily as he was, he couldn't allow her in.

'A man of mystery.' She tried to hide her smile by taking a bite of her food.

'Don't you think mystery is important?'

'No,' she answered honestly. 'It means keeping secrets, and secrets ruin everything. Having to keep the truth of my relationship with Lincoln a secret cost me my friends, and a great deal of my happiness. So, no, I don't care for mystery. Give me honesty, let me understand you, and I'll never betray your trust.'

Julian agreed with her. But the truth required more faith and trust in people than he was capable of giving. And he hadn't been happy for a long time. Most of his life. At the very best he had snapshots of it when he was younger. A taste of what he couldn't hold on to. Something to crave and miss and make him bitter.

'When did your father make this deal with Harrison?'

'When I was nineteen. I was in France when Arthur

died, and when I came back for the funeral my father told me what he had done. Lincoln seemed thrilled with the idea. I pleaded with my father to undo it, but I didn't want to displease him. I never did. Anyway, I went back to France to complete my studies…'

'You escaped.'

'I did.' Lily nodded. 'I was really grateful for the time I had left on my course, and the apprenticeship after that. I loved France, and I think I appreciated it even more after going back.'

'Do you miss it?'

'So much. On cold days we would all find a warm bistro and complain about the chefs at the school.' She chuckled with a faraway look in her eye. 'When it was warmer, we would fill up a pavement café.'

Julian couldn't help feeling caught up in her memories. The smile she wore now shone brighter than any other he'd seen her wear.

'Things felt simpler there,' she went on. 'I wasn't Lily Barnes-Shah. I didn't have to live up to anything or fulfil anyone's promise. I could just cook.' She looked up at Julian, her sadness evident now. 'I love being here. I wouldn't want to live anywhere else. Crème is my life. But I sometimes wish I could go back to Paris. Pretend I'm still in a time when my father was alive and not arranging a marriage I didn't want. When my mother was still willing to be there for me. When Devan and I were closer. It's ridiculous, isn't it?'

Julian pushed his empty bowl away, leaning forward on his folded elbows. 'It's not ridiculous to wish things were different. It just doesn't help you to deal with what's actually in front of you.'

'Have you ever wished that?'

It was such an innocent question, but to answer would force Julian to reveal more than he wanted to. And yet he wanted to tell her.

'My father wasn't a particularly wealthy man, but he was smart.'

He felt a burn scratch at the back of his throat, like it often had when he was younger. It had made him feel so weak that he had eventually stopped himself from thinking about Conrad Ford at all.

'He was a professor of robotics in LA.'

'What was he like?' Lily was leaning in, and without thinking he pulled her hand towards him, wrapping his strong fingers around hers.

'I don't know,' he answered. 'He died when I was two. I have no memory of him. He feels a bit like some mythological creature I can't be sure existed. Except—'

'Except of course he did, because you're here.'

Julian nodded. 'I was told that he was almost single-mindedly driven. But also a family man.'

'Brilliant and driven?' Lily summed up. 'Like father like son.'

'That's how it would seem.'

And Julian was certain that was precisely one of the reasons that his stepfather had hated him.

'Do you know what he looked like?' she asked.

He huffed a humourless laugh. 'You could be looking at him now.'

'Oh, Julian. I'm sorry.'

He batted away her apology, but he could see the sincerity on her face. There wasn't pity there—just a deep sadness on his behalf.

'You mentioned you had a stepfather, though...'

He tensed, but Lily's free hand coming up to draw lazy circles on top of his had the tension melting away.

'My mother remarried a few years later and we moved to Lupine Heights.'

Lily's brows rose. Clearly she had heard about the small town just outside LA and all the things he'd had to avoid growing up in that place. The crime, the drugs, the gangs...

'We lived there until she got cancer, and within a few months she was dead.'

'Oh, my God...'

He gave her a small smile. 'That's life. You can wish things to be different, but at the end of the day it doesn't matter because it's all temporary.'

Her face softened. 'Is that when you came up with your energy storage invention?'

Julian saw right through what she was attempting to do. But he was grateful for the change of topic because he didn't understand why he was talking to her about his past. All the things he kept hidden. The only person alive who knew about this was Henry, and that was because he had needed to know what he was taking on in a mentee.

'It is. I was fifteen at the time. I knew I could make money from selling it, but I didn't want to. It was mine, and I was going to make more money from keeping it and using it myself.'

'That's really impressive,' Lily said.

Her heart was breaking at all that he had revealed and everything he wasn't saying. But he was opening up to her just a little, so she would take what he offered.

'Why that invention?' she asked. 'Why renewable energy at all?'

'You mean besides it being good business? Because I've experienced enough of people trying to destroy the world without thought about who it affects. What will we have left if we keep taking without care?'

Lily could see him so clearly. This real version of him that he kept hidden beneath so many layers. He wore his ruthlessness like a badge of honour, but beneath that veil was a man who was trying to protect a world that she could tell had been cruel to him. She wouldn't say it out loud, though. Something told her he would deny it if she did.

This man had a beautiful heart. She had seen glimpses of it before. Now she was certain it was there. He just protected it with impenetrable armour.

And that was when she realised that she was in serious danger of falling for her fake fiancé.

Lily stared into those soulful, heartbroken eyes, not realising she been leaning closer and closer to him until a large hand wrapped around the side of her neck. His thumb stroked her cheek, making her rise with him as he stood, moving into her space beside the table. The hand on her neck skated along to grasp her chin, and his thumb caressed her lips before sinking to her mouth. She flicked her tongue against the pad, watching Julian's gaze become stormy. He pulled his thumb free, trailing it over her bottom lip. She closed her eyes. A shiver racked her body. Julian was so close his breath ghosted over her lips.

'I want to kiss you,' he whispered.

Say no.

'Please…' she breathed.

But he didn't. Not immediately at least. She stood there, head tilted up to his. His face so close. Tasting the air between them. The only contact: his fingers holding her chin. She felt possessed, but it didn't bother her. Oh no, she craved more. Then, as if he understood what she couldn't say, couldn't ask for, he touched his lips to hers, spreading a liquid warmth through her that pooled in her belly.

Softly, gently, his lips stroked hers. Caressed hers. Sending wave after wave of scalding pleasure over her. But she wanted more. Julian was making her wait. Taking his time. Giving her so much, but only releasing it as he wished to. Warm, wet bites had her moaning in desperation. Begging.

And then he gave her a little more. His free hand moved to her hip. Fingers dug into soft red fabric and flesh alike as he drew her flush against his body. His heat was engulfing her. She savoured the hardness of him. That coiled wildness held at bay by an iron will.

And then he slid his tongue into her mouth and she ignited. She wasn't aware of anything but Julian's mouth now. Couldn't control her body.

Smooth, silky strands flowed between her fingers and she realised she was tugging on his hair. A deep groan rumbled in his throat and his kisses grew harder, his tongue urgent. Demanding. The hands on her hip and chin disappeared and she was being lifted into the air, but she didn't open her eyes to see where they were going. She couldn't bear to. All she cared about was keeping her hands around his neck and their mouths fused together.

She heard a door close. The office door. They were in her office. Away from prying eyes. Completely alone.

This wasn't part of the show. This was for them. She should stop it, but she couldn't. She couldn't think of anything except that she burned for Julian.

Solid earth materialised under her feet, but it didn't matter because Julian was kissing her even more furiously now. Like a starving man having been denied food all his life finally finding nourishment. Her heaving breaths were rapid, and yet still she had no air. Her body was trembling. And even though she matched the ferocity of Julian's kisses, it wasn't enough.

'Julian…'

Was his name a plea or a prayer? She didn't know—but he did. Her back met the wall. She felt his thigh between her legs, propping her up, his hands skating over her breasts, his thumbs teasing her nipples. Lily moaned loudly. Sensation arrowed through her. Making her hips grind against him. She had never done this with a man before…

'Good girl,' he growled into her ear, before his teeth grazed the lobe.

His crazed, open-mouthed kisses covered her neck, her shoulder, and never once did his hands leave her breast. Hoarse moans and mewls flowed from her. And then without warning his hands dropped to her thighs and suddenly hoisted her up. She gasped as her sex pressed against the force of his hardness. It was the first time she had ever felt such a thing.

Her virginity was not something she held on to as some sort of treasure, rather that Lily hadn't wanted the intimacy when she was younger and definitely didn't want it with Lincoln, but now she found herself wishing Julian would take it.

She looked down at him through her lashes just as he was looking up at her through his.

Caught.

They were caught in a trap of their own making. The beast in him seemed barely tethered as he ground his hips against her, making her pulse race. Climbing to a height but she wasn't afraid of the fall. She craved it.

'Give it to me, Lily.'

His voice was low. Gravelly. Strangled. Raw.

And then she shattered. Plummeting through pleasure the like of which she had never known before. And Julian was kissing her again, until suddenly she found herself on his lap in a chair with no idea of how she'd got there.

He held her until her senses returned, and with it her voice of reason.

What had she done?

She had lost control so spectacularly. Lily couldn't think of a thing to say.

He dropped a kiss on her head and she had to hold in a sigh. This felt so good. Why shouldn't she indulge in whatever this was? She hadn't ever experienced attraction like this.

'I made dessert…' she said, and half laughed.

'I think that was it.' He kissed her neck. 'It's late.'

Lily nodded. They both needed a bit of space after what had happened. She got off his lap and saw his jaw tick as she left her office. She didn't know what he was thinking. Didn't know if he already regretted what had happened.

She cleared the table before he could emerge from the office, and once he did she locked up and allowed him to walk her to her car. When he kissed her cheek she hated it that she didn't know if it was part of their ruse or something more. The lines were blurred now.

She drove away thinking that even if this was a mistake, she couldn't bring herself to regret it.

CHAPTER EIGHT

THE LAST CUSTOMER had left Crème, and even though it was still bright outside Lily was happy to close up for the day. She had already sent everyone else home and the place was spotless—though one table in particular kept calling her attention. All day it had distracted her with flashes of the night before. Snippets of conversation playing over in her mind.

The world thought it knew about Julian, but hearing him speak of his mother and father had been something she wasn't prepared for. The matter-of-fact way he'd discussed them might have fooled most people, but not her. She was beginning to understand him, and she recognised that using his detached tone was the only way he could work around his sorrow.

She tried to imagine his loneliness. Tried to picture what it would have been like if her father had died when she was young, if she had lost her mother... But she couldn't because back then she'd still have had Devan.

She was starting to understand, though. Her mother's phone call was a wound that still throbbed, and yet she still had Julian—regardless of what they might be to each other.

It was surprising how much he cared. Which was

made even more clear by the reasons he'd got into his business.

Lily walked into her office to switch off her laptop. She glanced at the wall, feeling her cheeks heat immediately. She really needed to guard her heart with Julian. It was becoming far too easy to forget her reasons for doing this.

With her laptop bag slung over her shoulder, she locked up the office before returning to the front of the store.

'Lily.'

She jumped, dropping her bag. Her heart nearly beat out of her chest.

'Lincoln, you gave me a fright,' she said, trying to get her pulse under control. 'What are you doing here?'

It was a fair question. He hadn't ever visited her store, always claiming he was too busy, which had pleased Lily as Crème was the place she was happiest. Where she didn't have to be reminded of promises made and broken. There was no reason he would come here at all.

'I didn't mean to scare you,' he said, taking a step towards her. 'I just came here to talk.'

'Okay…' Lily said uncertainly.

'You know what this is about.'

He fished his phone out of his pocket and handed it to her. On the screen was a picture from the night before, of her and Julian having dinner, and another of their kiss. It felt wrong to have that embrace splashed about. Especially after all they had shared.

Lily handed the phone back, her engagement ring twinkling in the light, and Lincoln snatched her wrist to get a better look at it.

'What are you doing, Lily?'

She could hear how angry he was.

'I'm doing exactly what I want to. Marrying Julian. I love him, Linc.' She pulled her hand away from his and took a step back.

His blue eyes grew frigid. 'You love him?' he sneered. 'You can't be that naïve. He's using you to get to me—and, in case you've forgotten, you will be marrying me.'

Lily tried to remain calm. She wasn't afraid of Lincoln and she wasn't going to give him the satisfaction of getting angry. 'I won't be. I have chosen the man I want.'

'We had an agreement,' he spat.

'No, we didn't. *You* had an agreement with my father, but he's dead now and your arrangement should be too. I'm not anyone's property.'

In a flash, Lincoln's hand was wrapped around her arm, his grip nearly bruising. 'You're mine! Do you understand?'

'You're hurting me.'

'You're going to take off his ring. People expect us to be together. I won't have you embarrassing me.'

His teeth were clenched. There was a wild look in his eyes.

'People expect us to be together because you let them think that. You didn't have to agree to this madness.'

And for that Lily would never forgive him. She wasn't a trinket to be given or owned. She was a successful businesswoman with a first-rate education.

'Stop. Being. Stubborn,' said Lincoln. 'You're leaving with me.'

'I suggest you take your hands off her right now.'

Lily nearly sagged with relief at hearing that low, smooth voice dripping with fury. Rage had turned Julian's eyes more vividly green than she had ever seen them. She didn't know why he was here, she was just happy that he was.

Julian looked at the hand around Lily's arm, and then at the man holding her in place. A blistering rage overcame him. He wanted to rip into Lincoln. Tear him away from Lily. Only violence would satisfy his fury.

'Ford.' Lincoln curled his lip. 'This doesn't concern you.'

His muscles coiled beneath his expensive suit, Julian prowled towards them. 'You're touching what's mine. It very much concerns me.'

He stepped between Lily and Lincoln, prising his hand off her using a deathly grip that had Lincoln blanching.

'Leave. While you still can,' he growled.

Because if he didn't Julian was certain that Lincoln would only be leaving in the back of an ambulance. The image of another bloodied and broken man on a stretcher came to his mind, but this time Julian wouldn't feel a shred of guilt for putting him there.

At university it had taken him one moment to lose control—one snap of his temper to get his fists flying. He had been so far gone in his anger that he didn't remember a great deal of what had occurred. What he did remember was the satisfying connection of his fist, over and over again, with the guy's face and body. Pummelling him. Seeing the blood coating his own knuckles and shirt.

It had taken Henry's intervention to smooth things

over. Julian had got lucky. But his mentor had made sure he had another outlet for his rage after that, and Julian had recognised the violence he was capable of.

Now, both men stared each other down, but with Julian shielding Lily, he would not be the one to cave. He hadn't meant to call her his, but now that the words had left his lips he liked the way it had sounded. Lily *was* his.

In those extra minutes he'd needed after she'd left the office last night, he'd realised how consumed he was with her. Which was dangerous to his goals. To his need for control. That was why he'd come here now. To make sure she understood that nothing further could come from what they had shared. That he had Arum and Zenith to consider. Neither of them was looking for more. That wasn't part of their agreement. He'd wanted to have that conversation in person. Now he was thankful for deciding to do that.

Lincoln spun on his heel and left.

Only once the door had slowly swung closed did Julian turn around. He took Lily's face in his hands, lowering himself to look into her eyes. 'Are you hurt?'

'No. No, I'm fine,' she reassured him.

'Let me see.'

He pushed her sleeve up to see light red bands on her tanned skin. His breathing grew ragged.

'Julian, I'm fine,' she said, touching his cheek. 'Look, they're already fading.'

'Don't worry, baby, I'm fine.'

He flinched at the memory. He wasn't going to let that happen again. Not to Lily. He would protect her from everyone.

'I'm moving up our timetable. You're moving in with me now.'

'Julian…'

'You're not safe alone, Lily.'

His voice had still not returned to its normal register.

'I'm not afraid of Lincoln. I refuse to be. I've known him my whole life. I think we should stick to the plan.'

Julian stood to his full height, settled on his decision. 'If you don't move in with me tonight, I will just have to take you everywhere you need to go personally, and I will be hiring a security team that will shadow your every move. Up to you, sunshine.'

He knew she would never go for that. He was forcing her to pick the only acceptable option. Even though he would have to figure out how he would keep her at arm's length when she was under his roof.

'This is a gross overreaction,' she told him. 'You do realise that, right?'

Defiance burned in those obsidian eyes.

'One way or another, I will keep you safe. Now, you can come with me, or I can rearrange my entire life for as long as we are together.'

'You're impossible! Fine. I'll move in with you.'

'Tonight, Sunshine.'

'You really are one to close every loophole, aren't you? Yes, tonight. Now. Let's go.'

Julian sat behind the steering wheel of Lily's car while she furiously texted her brother. After having his own car sent home, he'd insisted on going with her to fetch her possessions—which surprisingly hadn't taken long. Devan hadn't been home, and when Lily had tried to call she'd reached his PA.

Julian had helped her load her bags into her car and she'd handed over the keys, saying she had to let her brother know what was happening.

'He's not happy,' Lily said, staring down at her phone.

Of course he wouldn't be.

He would have likely already heard about Lincoln's visit.

'He thinks I'm making a mistake.'

'He'll come around, Lily.'

Julian couldn't explain his need to constantly reassure her. Make her happy. He needed to get a hold of himself—especially if they were to live together.

'And even if he doesn't, at least you will be able to live on your terms. You don't need his permission or his blessing.'

'No, I don't,' she agreed.

But he heard the note of sadness in her tone and hated it. He had grown to care for her beaming smiles, even though he knew they covered up a world of hurt. And the fact that he craved them told him that he was growing far too attached.

He lived alone for a reason.

He rounded a corner onto a road lined with lush green from its grassy, well-manicured pavements to the hedges and tall trees. The houses here were large and stood close together. Except his. It was the only property with land to spare on either side. The trees almost completely blocked the house from sight.

'I didn't expect this much privacy here,' Lily said as the gate swung wide and he drove down a short driveway to an underground garage, where he parked her car next to his and killed the engine.

Thinking it was the perfect opportunity to show Lily who he was, and stop her from getting closer, Julian turned to face her. 'I bought the houses next to mine and razed them.'

He saw shock, maybe a little horror on her face, and climbed out of the car just before she did. She did not wait for him to open her door, which annoyed him. He got her bags and Lily followed close behind, as if she was trying to process what he'd said.

'Just to have the land?' she finally asked, sounding scandalised.

'To be alone,' Julian responded simply.

To have peace.

'Why not just buy elsewhere?'

Julian placed her bags on the floor and walked out onto a terrace that overlooked the cliff face and the water below. He could feel Lily behind him.

'Because this is what I wanted, and I make damned sure I get what I want.'

'Why?'

She wasn't asking why he went after he wanted— he was certain she already understood that from their conversations. No, this question begged to know why *here*. It revealed only her curiosity, but an answer from him would reveal so much more.

Julian looked at her but said nothing as he picked up her bags and walked away, leaving her outside. He climbed the glass staircase. There was so much glass in his home. The Bay was visible from virtually every spot in the house. Julian loved being alone here, where he could breathe.

Lily fell into step beside him, not saying a word. He

pushed open a door and gestured for her to enter first. Apart from his room, this was the room he loved most.

There was a wash basin and large tub in the corner beside a low wall that offered both privacy and a breathtaking view through the massive window that angled into the room turning the ceiling into a wide rectangular strip. The king-sized bed sat on a plush carpet, the headboard against a wood-panelled wall. The view of the sky uninterrupted from the bed. An ever-changing work of art.

'Closet is through those doors,' he said, setting her bags on the bed.

'Thank you, Julian. It's beautiful.'

He watched her walk to the window, looking out with a small smile on her face.

'Would you like me to send for the rest of your things?'

'That's not necessary.' She spun around and stepped around him to place a miniature Eiffel Tower on the bedside table. 'I have everything I need.'

Was he expected to believe that this woman who had grown up with such excess was going to live out of two suitcases?

She must have seen the scepticism on his face because she said, 'I have Crème, and I'm on the verge of getting my freedom. I don't need anything else.'

The words resonated too deeply with him. Because wasn't that his life too? What this place was meant to represent? IRES and freedom.

IRES had given him wealth and power, and that had given him freedom. Freedom to leave his past behind… freedom to create this sanctuary…freedom to live his life any way he damn well pleased.

'Join me downstairs when you're ready.'

He turned on his heel, leaving the room before he did something foolish. Because all he could think of was how much he would rather have her sleeping in *his* bed. Something he'd never wanted before.

Julian felt conflicted over having her in his home. He was maddeningly attracted to her, but having another person in his space had him ill at ease. And yet he still wanted to spend every moment with her, protect her… Which had him gritting his teeth.

He couldn't want that. He never wanted that kind of chaos in his life. He found peace in his home and Lily affected that far too much. He needed to take back control. Not let his affection for her grow. Because he had seen what loving someone, letting them in, could do to a person. Had seen his mother suffer day after day.

Needing a moment to clear his head, Julian stepped out on the terrace, taking a deep breath and focussing on his plan instead. Having royally angered Lincoln, Julian knew he had to find the insurance he needed to trump Lincoln's vote—but now he didn't just want to do it for his plan. Seeing the man's hand on Lily had Julian craving retribution, but he knew now he'd have to work harder on Devan.

He pulled out his phone and made the call.

'Shah,' he greeted him.

'What are you doing?' Devan demanded, not bothering to conceal his anger.

'I'm sure I don't know what you're talking about,' Julian said smoothly.

'Making Lily move in with you. You're using her.'

'I think you're projecting.'

'What?'

The word was a low threat that did nothing to move Julian.

'This arranged marriage to keep the power at Arum between you and Harrison. Here's the thing… When I walk in to find Lincoln Harrison manhandling my fiancée, I tend to become somewhat unreasonable.'

'Lincoln hurt Lily?'

Just like that the man's anger disappeared, to be replaced by a concern that made Julian want to laugh. How concerned could her brother truly be if Lily was having to move into *his* home?

'I could show you the marks if you'd like,' he said. But provoking Devan further wouldn't help, so he softened his tone. 'Lily is safe with me, Devan. I can protect her. Always will.'

That wasn't a lie. Even after all this was over and they were nothing to each other he would still protect her.

'I just thought you should know.'

There was a pause on the line before Devan responded. 'Thank you for telling me.' It seemed like he wanted to say more, but instead he said, 'I'll be keeping an eye.'

'I'd wonder what kind of brother you were if you didn't.'

Julian ended the call and slid the phone into his pocket. Devan should have seen the marks on Lily. He knew it wasn't serious but it did nothing to quell his rage.

Being around Lily made memories surface that he worked every single day to forget. But he would never forget.

Blood and bruises. Who could forget that?

Julian wanted to protect Lily. Except he knew his feelings didn't stop at protection. He could barely exercise restraint around her. The night before had proved that much.

There was only one thing he could really do. Pretend to be her doting fiancé in public but keep his distance at home.

The first thing that had struck Lily about Julian's home was how tranquil it was. It was so silent that she could barely hear the sounds of waves lapping on the shore. She could see why he would have wanted this place, but it had taken her more than a moment to get over the shock of him ruthlessly tearing down houses to get it.

And he was ruthless.

To buy a home, with all its memories, and then raze it... She couldn't imagine it. It seemed callous. And that was a part of Julian. Yet it seemed at odds with the person she was discovering him to be.

It was something she should try to remember.

He kept his eyes fixed on his goal and she would have to as well.

She made her way downstairs and found Julian standing out on the terrace, hands in his pockets, face turned up to a sky not quite dark enough to see any stars. He was so utterly, heartbreakingly beautiful. She could see in the set of his shoulders and in the expression on his face that for once his guard was down, and it allowed her to glimpse the sadness within him.

There was more to his story. She wasn't naïve enough to think he had confided in her about his whole life, but what he had said was already more than any child should bear. Maybe that was exactly what had sowed the seed of callousness in him. She couldn't imagine what else he had been through. What had scarred his soul.

Yet, even so, his determination was clear in every part of him. Those suits and his perfect appearance did nothing to hide that barely leashed power, and she wondered what would set it free.

She stepped out to join him, felt goosebumps rising in the chill breeze coming off the Bay. Julian shrugged off his jacket and draped it around her shoulders. His warmth was already so familiar.

'Settled?' he asked.

'As well as can be expected.' She walked up to the railing, seeing the startlingly blue infinity pool below her and the beach far below that. 'You have a beautiful home. So light. Airy…'

'I sense a question there.'

'I just didn't expect it.' She hadn't seen drapes or blinds on any of the windows. 'I guess I'm wondering why. You are so private and this is so very open.'

'Because when you've spent your whole life in the dark, Lily, all you do is crave light. How's your arm?'

'My arm? Oh, fine.' She had almost forgotten about Lincoln altogether, even though he was the reason she was here.

'He won't get away with it.' Julian joined her, resting his elbows on the railing as he gazed over the water. 'I'll make sure he pays for hurting you. I made you a promise.'

Lily was struck that he should want to protect her so ferociously from the one person who held what he really wanted. It made her feel she was a priority. Not something she was used to.

'No,' she said, and he turned to look at her. 'Don't

do anything that could hurt you later—and I'm not just talking about the Arum deal.' A boldness gripped her, and she placed her hand over his heart. 'Some things are more important.'

His eyes shifted into softness, which then morphed into something scorching, before all emotion was cleared away and he pulled away from her, stalking inside, leaving her feeling unbalanced.

She was growing to care deeply for Julian. Especially after what had happened on their date at Crème. But maybe she was reading the situation all wrong. After all, he was far more experienced than her. Maybe for him it was nothing more than a physical reaction and she was overstepping.

Why was it so much harder for her to remember the fake part of their relationship?

Lily lay in bed, staring at the sky as it was transformed from a black void to a blue and gold painting of sunrise. She threw off the covers and changed into her work clothes, despite it being so early, because she couldn't remain in this room any longer.

She took a look around the house, noticing the absence of anything sentimental. There were no knick-knacks nor any indication of childhood memories, no pictures on the walls save for artistic photographs clearly purchased at a gallery. It was all so careful not to hint at the past. As if all that mattered to Julian was right now.

She went down to the kitchen, wondering if he would soon join her, but she found a note on the countertop saying he had an early meeting and wouldn't be back until later.

The note didn't sit well with her. Surely he would

have mentioned the meeting the night before or knocked on her door earlier.

There was a nagging voice in the back of her mind telling her that he was avoiding her.

He didn't have any reason to, did he?

She got her answer later, after she'd arrived back at his home, having heard nothing from him all day. It was just a simple text saying he was tied up at the office and wouldn't be back before dinner.

He was definitely avoiding her.

He couldn't have gone from wanting to rearrange his entire life to being so busy he barely had time for meals that weren't at his office. Something was going on, and she was determined to find out what it was.

She waited up, finally hearing him enter late into the night.

'Welcome home,' Lily said, stepping into the light of his open-plan kitchen.

'Lily. What are you doing up?' He gave her the barest of glances before placing a cup down on the counter.

'Waiting for you.' She saw his eyes close momentarily, a tick in his jaw. 'We need to talk.'

'Whatever it is, I'm sure it can wait.'

'No, it can't. I want to know what I've done to make you avoid me.'

Her voice was strong. Whatever his answer was, she was resolved not to be hurt by it. There was a problem and they needed to fix it.

'I'm not avoiding you,' he said impatiently, placing his hands on the counter on either side of his cup.

'That's the first lie you've told that I genuinely don't believe.'

'I don't know what you want me to tell you.'

'The truth. Why are you avoiding me?' She stood beside him now, not giving him the chance to evade her.

'Lily...' he growled.

'We're doing this thing that requires us to be honest with each other, Julian. I'm not backing down until you tell me what's going on.' When he did nothing but heave a frustrated sigh, Lily pushed. 'Is it because I'm here? Do you regret it?'

'*Yes*, damn it!'

Lily recoiled as though she had been slapped.

Julian pushed away from the counter, running his fingers through his thick red hair as he stepped away from her before whipping around, fire in his eyes.

'Do you know what you do to me?' he almost yelled. 'You make me want to lose control!'

Lily was stunned. The words sent sparks through her body. She'd thought she had done something wrong. Something to push him away. But she was wrong. He also felt whatever was building between them, and it wasn't just attraction.

'Then do it,' she said evenly, standing her ground.

Julian stared at her, a scorching look in his eyes. 'You don't know what you're saying,' he said slowly.

Lily lifted her chin. Every bit the confident Shah she'd been raised to be. 'Maybe I do.'

Julian stalked towards her, barely restrained, grabbing her arms in a vice-like grip. 'You have no idea.'

Lily thought of everything she knew about him. How much he wouldn't let out. Maybe he needed to. Maybe she could be the one he let go with.

She raised herself up on her toes and kissed him softly. An innocent touch before lightly licking his lip. 'Show me.'

'Lily…' he groaned.

She could feel the tension in his muscles.

'Julian…' she whispered, and he seized her mouth.

Lifting her onto the counter, he stepped between her legs and she wrapped them around him. He held her face as his teeth tugged at her lip, making her gasp. Lily had thought their other kisses had set her aflame, but they were nothing on this. His control was in tatters. His need was speaking to hers, turning into an all-consuming storm with both of them in the centre of it.

There was nothing gentle about this kiss. Nothing gentle about the grip he had on her or her fingers pressing into his back under his jacket. There was no masking the sounds of want he made, in conversation with her own moans. But just as quickly as his lips were on her, he was yanking himself away, his chest rapidly rising and falling.

'Not like this,' he said. He moved back, pressing his forehead against hers. 'Not like this.'

'Julian, I want—'

'Tomorrow I'm taking you on a date.'

Her heart fell. 'Our third date…'

CHAPTER NINE

THAT EVENING LILY made sure she was home early. Having no idea where Julian was taking her, she paced back and forth in the walk-in closet. To be honest, she was rather unsettled by this date. After Julian's admission, and that kiss that had felt so real, she'd thought they were making progress to something more. Something she'd realised in that moment she desperately wanted.

She had made the first move. Had felt liberated enough to decide for herself that she wanted Julian. Then he'd said he would be taking her on a date, and it had felt as if the rug had been pulled from under her.

Always their arrangement.

That was his shield, wasn't it? Whenever he was pushed into real feelings, Julian put those walls back up. And while Lily had no illusions of what this was meant to be, no one could have predicted their intense chemistry.

Maybe she just had to be patient.

She pulled her satin robe tighter, taking another look through the racks.

'Lily?' Julian's voice came through the door.

She pulled it open, revealing him in a black suit, his

hair just slightly damp. The scent of leather and spice wove around her. She gestured him to enter the room, which was generously sized, but with him in it suddenly felt very confined. Especially with his eyes trailing over her robe and then moving back up to her face. The unmistakable flare of want was there.

'Can you tell me where we're going?' she asked.

He cleared his throat. 'That's why I'm here.' He reached into his jacket pocket, revealing two tickets that he handed to her. Her eyes widened when she read them.

'How…?' she breathed. 'It's been sold out for months.'

His fingers grazed over her cheek. 'When are you going to learn? There's nothing I can't do.'

A smile stretched across her face. He was taking her to a French play that she had wanted to see so badly, but the tickets had been snapped up before she'd even had a chance to buy one. Lily had consoled herself by saying it was for the best, because she would have had to attend alone.

'Happy?' he asked tenderly.

'Yes! So happy!' She hugged him tightly, trying to convey how much this meant to her. 'Thank you, Julian.'

'You don't have to thank me, Sunshine.'

'I guess I should get ready.'

She pulled away and Julian caught her around her nape pressing a quick kiss to her lips. 'You can keep those.'

He left the room, leaving Lily holding the tickets and trying to keep tears at bay. He had understood how much she had loved her time in France. Understood what this would mean to her. This might be a fake relationship, but no one had ever treated Lily like this. As if what she said and loved mattered in a massive way.

* * *

Julian waited at the foot of stairs, his nose buried in an email that he was replying to without paying much attention. He really had wanted to keep his distance from Lily, but when she'd pushed, leaving his precious control in pieces, he'd realised he couldn't stay away. He didn't want to.

He wanted her. He wanted her more than he wanted anything else. And while he didn't deserve her, he could enjoy what they had while it lasted. Why shouldn't he? Everything came to an end. Everything was taken away at some point. So until then he would soak up all he could from her and then, when it was done, he would tuck those memories away with all the others he tried never to think about.

That was why he'd had to stop that kiss. Lily deserved more than a frantic, lust-filled ravishing on a kitchen countertop. She deserved to be taken care of, to be worshipped—which was why he'd bought those tickets to the play. It had stung when she'd assumed it was another date for their arrangement, but it was good because she wouldn't allow herself to get too close to him.

The click of a heel was the first thing he heard. Slipping his phone into his pocket, he looked up. His breath caught. How was it possible that this woman wanted him? She was perfect.

Thin purple straps sat on tanned shoulders. The neckline of her dress dipped into a V in the valley of her breasts. The skirt was gathered at her tiny waist before falling to the floor in layers of rich purple chiffon. There was a long slit up her left leg, and he could see flashes as she stepped onto the stair below. Her hair was pulled up, and he could almost taste the skin at her neck.

'Exquisite.' He held out a hand to help her down, revelling in her glorious smile.

'You don't look too bad yourself, Ford.'

He flashed a smile at her—something he found himself doing more frequently these days—and led her to the car, sneaking glances at her all the way on their drive to the theatre.

When they finally took their seats in gold and red opulence, Julian lifted their threaded fingers to his lips. It wasn't enough.

'So, are you going to require a translator?' Lily teased.

He chuckled. 'I'll manage.'

'Good, because I can't promise that I would remember.'

Julian knew he would try his best to remember this moment. Her unguarded happiness. He heard the play start, caught glimpses of it, but all that really held his attention was the woman beside him. Every emotion was displayed on her face, and yet, throughout, that smile never wavered.

His thumb stroked across her knuckles and he leaned over to kiss her hair. And then, almost without realising it, he was on his feet, clapping with everyone else as the cast took a bow and the curtain fell.

A tear fell from her eye, kissing her cheek before falling. He brushed it away with the back of his finger, proud that he could have brought her to something that had moved her so deeply.

'Did you enjoy that?' he asked.

Lily nodded enthusiastically. 'So much. You don't know what this means to me.'

'Come on.'

He led her out of the theatre, avoiding anyone who might want to speak to them, ignoring the unmistakeable flashes of a camera, and helped her into his waiting car.

Tipping the valet, he slid into the driver's seat and turned to Lily. Not quite ready to put an end to the night when she looked so happy, Julian asked, 'Would you like to take a drive with me?'

'I'd love that.'

They drove along the darkened streets in comfortable silence. Words were unneeded for whatever was passing between them…building between them.

It wasn't long before they were meandering through the winding roads of Golden Gate Park. Vibrant green foliage illuminated by his headlights flashed by, and soon he parked at the side of the road, climbed out, and rounded the front of the car to assist Lily, before taking her hand and walking over the bridge.

The bright full moon was their only source of light, casting a silvery glow on everything it touched. It was enough to see where they were going, but Julian still scooped Lily up in his arms as if she weighed nothing and set off on the path.

'What are you doing?' She laughed.

'Saving you a twisted ankle.'

It was an excuse, and they both knew it, but she let it drop.

Julian had, of course, been to Strawberry Hill before. He had seen couples and families walking the paths or sailing in the paddle boats and he'd never understood. Not until now. When he had someone special to appreciate this place with.

A pagoda with bright red pillars and a jade roof appeared at the water's edge and Julian set Lily on her feet once he'd climbed the stairs and stood at the stone banister.

'It's so beautiful out here…and quiet,' Lily said, leaning into his warmth.

Julian wrapped an arm around her shoulders, pulling her against his side, tipping her head up to kiss her just once.

'Cold?'

She shook her head and gazed out at Stow Lake, but his gaze was firmly on her. As it had been all night.

'I know I've already said it, but thank you for tonight.'

She looked up at him and he was lost in those bottomless eyes that seemed as if they could hold an entire universe.

'My family used to go to the theatre together when I was younger,' she said.

He could tell it was a happy memory. It was clear from the longing in her voice. 'You miss it,' he stated.

'I do. I used to be so close to my father… I thought he was perfect in every way. I think we were just a very close family—especially Devan and I—but this arranged marriage with Lincoln changed all that. My relationship with my father wasn't ever the same. It became…'

'Strained?' Julian offered.

'Yes. And it was like that until he died. I wish we could have fixed things. It's the one regret I have. But I'm also so angry with him. Angry that he promised me to Lincoln. Angry that he died before he could fulfil his promise to me to undo it. Angry because I feel like he didn't do all that he could, and now I have all this anger towards Devan and my mother.'

'It's okay to feel that way, Lily. The people who should have protected you didn't. You have every right to be angry.' Julian shook his head, thinking of how everyone responded to her. All those bright smiles in her store. 'You have no reason to treat everyone as kindly as you do. This world has failed you.'

'No, it hasn't. *You* haven't.' She smiled at him. 'I know I have the right to feel betrayed and angry, but I don't want to live my life under a dark cloud. I refuse to. There are good people in this world too, so I choose to see the best where I can.'

Like she did with him. But would she still think so when she knew of the darkness in his heart? Why he didn't let himself love?

He found himself talking before he'd consciously thought about the words. Words he hadn't uttered in years. Maybe ever.

'The man my mother married was an alcoholic. I don't remember much of our lives in LA after my father died, but I do remember the day we moved to Lupine Heights. I was six at the time, and from the moment we stepped into that small dark house I knew I didn't want to be there.'

Julian felt Lily's arms wrap around him, but he couldn't see her. All he could see was the stream of memories.

'From that first day I hated the way he looked at her, but I didn't understand it then. After their wedding his drinking got worse. It stopped being something that happened at night and became a constant. He was volatile at the best of times, but when he drank he was completely out of control. My mother tried to please him. Keep him happy. Hoping that if she made things easier for him he'd have no reason to turn that volatility on us.'

He looked at Lily then. Hoping she would understand what he was saying. Why he wanted to help her so much. Protect her from Lincoln like he never could his mother.

'It was a ridiculous hope. The first time he hit her she made me hide in the closet, but I could hear, and when I couldn't take it any more I burst out and ran to her. She was cowering on the kitchen floor, and that was the first time I felt rage.'

He shook his head, trying to clear away the fear, the anger.

'I leapt at him, but I was just a kid and he easily slapped me aside. So I kneeled beside her...'

Don't worry, baby, I'm fine. He could still hear his mother's voice in his head. See her weak, tear-stained smile.

'It became a constant thing after that. And I tried to protect her, but I was weak. Eventually he had enough of me interfering and turned his violence on me.'

Julian still remembered the bruises. The pain of his broken arm.

'You weren't weak. You were young. Didn't anyone help you? Report him?'

Julian smiled serenely down at Lily, brushing her tears away and kissing her forehead.

'Who would?'

He was certain that the abuse had been suspected at his school, but no one had helped him, choosing instead to believe whatever lies his stepfather had told.

'He would just explain everything away. I begged my mother to leave, but she never did.'

Again, he hadn't been chosen.

'She tried to defend me, but that only put her in harm's way. There was no winning. And then, just before I turned fifteen, she died. It was his fault. He drank away every penny we had. There was nothing left for her treatment.'

And he had done nothing. It had just been him and his mother against the world and he had done nothing. How had his genius helped him then?

Guilt and shame ravaged him.

'When did it stop?' Lily asked, her voice hoarse and scratchy.

'For her? When she got sick. For me? After she died. He didn't realise how much bigger than him I'd had grown. I hadn't either, until one day he came at me, and I swung for him, and the next thing I knew he was across the room in a heap.'

He felt a phantom pain spread across his knuckles. Felt a savage satisfaction settling in his belly as if the wound was still fresh. He had enjoyed it then. Had got high on the power of beating his stepfather. It had been the first real slice of elation he had felt in years. That explosion of violence had made him happy, and he had known what he was because of it.

'What happened to him?'

He could see she was hoping for some retribution. He had wanted that too.

'Nothing. I graduated from high school early, studied on a full ride and never went back. I haven't seen him in over a decade. This is why I need control. Why

I don't have relationships or friends. I can't risk turning into him. I can't risk falling in love.'

'Julian,' she cried. 'Vincent is not your father. You are not him.'

'I don't remember my father, Lily. It doesn't matter what blood I have in me when that was the man who raised me. I'm vengeful because of him. I'm ruthless because of him. I watched my mother die because of him. All of that is in me. You say you want to see the good in people? Some of us don't have any good left.'

'That's not true.' Her hand caressed his cheek and he wiped away the tears that wouldn't stop. 'You're a good man, Julian. If you weren't, you wouldn't be helping me. Wouldn't have protected me from Lincoln. Wouldn't own the company you do. You're *good*.'

Julian took her face in his hands, lowering his lips to hers slowly. His eyes were on hers, and just as their lips touched her wet lashes fluttered closed, but his didn't. He couldn't bear not to look at her.

'Lily…' he whispered.

He wanted to devour her but he took his time savouring her, kissing her sweetly under the stars. Not a soul in sight. Just him and her and the give of her soft lips, salty with tears shed for him. A crack formed in his chest at that alone.

She grabbed the lapels of his jacket, pulling herself up, trying to be closer to him, so he lifted her, holding her tightly, letting her kiss him deeply, a little clumsily. Her inexperience endearing. And then he was pushing her back against a pillar, his tongue demanding. Wanting Lily to give him more. For her to seek out her most hidden desires and present it to him.

Furious.

That was what this kiss had become.

Mouths moving together.

Biting. Licking. Sucking.

Pleading.

And then Lily was whispering in his ear. 'Take me home, Julian.'

CHAPTER TEN

THEY BURST THROUGH the door of Julian's house. Lips frantic. Hands in hair, on chests, under shirts. No time to speak. No time to breathe.

His body was coiled, begging him to take her where they stood, but he wouldn't heed that call. There was only one place he wanted her.

He slid his hands under her thighs, through the slit in her dress, picking her up and walking up the stairs to his bedroom. Lily wouldn't let him stop kissing her, making his blood pound. He couldn't remember a time when a woman had driven him this crazy.

Julian took her into his bedroom, releasing a string of profanities as he let her slide down his body, bringing her to stand in front of him. He was painfully hard.

Holding Lily's heavy gaze, Julian trailed his fingers up the back of her neck to the elegant silver clip holding her hair up. As gently as he could, he pulled the long, shiny stick away from the barrette, dropping both pieces to the floor with a clatter. Her hair fell in a waterfall of luscious black. An oil spill over his light hands.

Doing the one thing he had wanted to since stepping into Crème, Julian wrapped the length of her hair around his hand, tugging her head back in a fist to expose her throat. He groaned, tasting the skin there.

Sweet. She was so damn sweet.

That flowery scent, with a hint of vanilla intoxicated him—it was almost as if the bakery had permanently etched itself into her skin.

He kissed her again. Slowly this time. Reverently.

'Julian…' she moaned. 'Stop teasing me.'

But he wasn't. He was driving himself mad. Wanting to take his time. To taste and kiss every inch of her. Discover her every secret. Find out if she would beg or plead or pray…

'Sunshine…' his voice was gruff '…tell me you want this.'

He needed to hear her say the words because he had never wanted something so badly in his life.

'I want this…' she breathed. 'Julian?'

'Hmm?' He was kissing the spot below her ear that had her melting in his arms.

'I have to tell you something first.'

He pulled away to look at her. At the serious look on her face. So uncertain…

He tugged on her chin. 'You can tell me anything.'

'I'm…' Her face turned crimson. 'I've never done this.'

He frowned, before understanding took hold. 'You're a virgin?'

She nodded, trying to look anywhere but at him. He'd known she was inexperienced. Could tell from her kisses. But he'd never once suspected she would be a virgin. Not especially with her being promised away. Christ, she never had a single moment to enjoy her life.

'Are you mad?' she asked.

He couldn't help but laugh. 'No, Sunshine. I'm not mad. I am very, *very* not mad.'

He smiled. A primitive part of him rejoiced.

Lily was his. His and his alone.

He was overcome with relief that he hadn't lost control the night before, and determined to make this night unforgettable for her.

Lily's face was on fire. Embarrassment was curling through her after having to admit her inexperience, but at the same time her heart was racing. Full to the point of bursting. Because she wanted this so badly and she wanted it with Julian.

His warm hand caressed her cheek and she leaned into the touch.

'Look at me,' he said.

She obeyed without thought.

'I'm glad you told me.'

His lips on her forehead sent a shiver down her body.

'And I'll offer you a first too.'

Lily looked at him, confused.

'I have never brought a woman here.'

'To your bedroom?'

'My home. Just you, Sunshine.'

Lily was so happy that she had waited. So happy that her first time could be with Julian. She realised how deeply she trusted him. And he trusted her too. If he didn't, he would never have told her everything he had tonight.

'Take me, Julian.'

She was jittery with anticipation. Excited and just a little scared of the unknown. He had already shown her pleasure once, and they had both been fully clothed. How would tonight change her?

He sucked her lip between his, sending tingles throughout her body, making her open to him, begging for him to deepen the kiss. But he didn't. She watched him step away and kick off his shoes and socks before standing before her.

'Undress me.'

The whispered command had her gasping. Excited to touch all the hardness that she had felt under his shirt. Every bit of him was accessible to her now. It was exhilarating.

She swallowed thickly, her gaze meeting his heated stare. A gentle smile of encouragement on his face. God! Those dimples were going to be the end of her.

Slipping her hand under his jacket, she saw Julian's eyes close, and he let out a slow exhale. She pushed his jacket off his shoulders, letting it fall, then trailed her fingers over the buttons of his perfect white shirt. Then a sudden impatience seized her and she couldn't wait. Grabbing the placket in her delicate fists, she looked at him, gave him a wicked smirk that he returned, and ripped it open, sending buttons popping and scattering all over his hardwood floor.

His eyes darkened even further. Lily hadn't known she could feel this wild…this uninhibited. This demanding of what she wanted. She tugged down his pants and his underwear with them. There was no waiting now. And when he kicked them aside she got to see him. *Really* see him.

Nothing could have prepared her for the wave of arousal she felt at the sight of his body. Lean. Muscular. Every muscle was carved into him as if he was made of marble. Power kept at bay by the silken veil that was his skin. Every inch honed perfection. And then there was the tattoos that had been hidden by his suits.

Bold and black and so striking against his fair skin, it wasn't a pretty piece, but she could tell it wasn't meant to be. It was a massive dying tree, with a knotted, twisted trunk and gnarled roots inked over his ribs and ending at his hip. Bare branches curled towards his nipple.

Lily traced the pattern with her fingers. Followed the branches as they curled and grew around his side towards his shoulder blade. The dead, barren branches slowly grew. Burls giving way to tiny leaves that became lush and full. From death to life. And on his left pec was a series of roman numerals separated with two little dots.

She noticed his breathing had become ragged. His lips were pressed together, studying her. She didn't want to think about what the tattoo meant. He had given her enough this night.

'Kiss me,' she ordered.

One arm wrapped around her waist and the other held the back of her head as he fused their mouths together, gliding his tongue over hers. Each swipe speared to her sex, making her gasp loudly. Then she felt his hands on the back of her dress, tugging the zip down until the fabric parted. She shivered when his fingers trailed lightly over her bare spine.

A groan coming from deep in his throat.

'So soft…' he said against her lips, peeling the dress away.

Her stomach fluttered as he scooped her up without warning and placed her in the centre of his massive bed, crawling over her exactly like the jungle cat she'd thought him to be the first time she saw him.

His lips trailed over her jaw, down her neck, over her chest…kissing, tasting, biting in a lightning trail that had her breathing hard. Lily hadn't ever felt anything like this. As if she was floating and drowning all at once. And then his mouth closed over her nipple and she arched off the bed but then Julian was running a hand down her side soothing and igniting at once. An earnest supplication of pleasure so intense it had to be sinful.

His lips returned to hers as his fingers trailed up the inside of her thigh, but he didn't stop there, easing her lace panties aside and stroking her sex. She knew how wet he would find her.

Lily had always assumed being this intimate with someone would be difficult, maybe even mortifying the first few times, but it wasn't. A voice at the back of her mind told her that Julian made the difference. She believed that she was safe with him. That he would take her pleasure and treasure it.

'I'm going to go slow…' He kissed her sweetly. 'You can stop at any point, Lily. Do you understand?'

She nodded.

'I need to hear you say the words, Sunshine.'

'I understand.'

'Good.'

He reached into a drawer in the nightstand and pulled out a foil square. He reared back and she watched him roll latex on his daunting length. She was suddenly nervous. Excited, but tense. Falling into her head were questions and possibilities, and it was Julian's teeth biting her lip that had her coming back to him.

'I'll take care of you, Lily.'

She watched him move to the foot of the bed, pulling off her underwear. She stopped breathing entirely when his mouth lowered to her sex. His tongue had her awash in sensation, her hips bucking to meet his mouth and a large arm curled around her, his hand pinning her to the bed, and he licked and sucked and soon had her drowning in a river of pleasure.

The bedding fisted in her palms, she uttered a melody of whimpering cries she had no capacity to understand as they filled the room.

Further and further away she was swept in this torrent. Her toes curled. Her body was his to control. She was relaxed, and yet strung impossibly taut, and as she begged him…*begged* for release…just before she could be taken over the edge she was in Julian's arms, foreheads connected, his hardness at her entrance for one eternal moment before he thrust into her and held her tightly.

A cry fell from her mouth and he kissed it away. Keeping still, he held her close until she could adjust to his large intrusion.

'You're okay, Sunshine. Take as long as you need.'

His voice didn't sound like his at all. It was strangled. Tense.

The burn faded quickly and she tried moving her hips, shocked at just how good it felt. So Julian began to move. Slowly at first. And then he bent her leg, which she wrapped around his hip, and she couldn't think. Couldn't breathe.

How could anything feel this good? It was killing her in the best possible way.

'Breathe, Lily,' he whispered in her ear, which only sent her soaring that much higher. 'You're incredible.'

She wanted to respond. Wanted to say something—anything. But there were no words in the world. There never would be. All that existed was Julian and how he made her feel.

She opened her eyes—that she had no idea when she had closed at all—to see their bodies joined, moving rhythmically together. Julian's body chorded, betraying the strength that lay in those muscles that treated her so gently. His light eyes—so dark—heated but there was something more than heat in them and her body pulled tight, caught in a raging torrent. Her pleasure crested until she crashed around him, shouting out his name as he grunted his own release.

Panting was the only sound in the silence.

She felt Julian's head in the crook of her neck, tried to stroke his hair but she was boneless.

Lily wasn't sure what she'd expected, but it certainly hadn't been this. Pleasure so intense that a tear fell from her eye, cutting a wet path down to her temple.

She felt Julian's lips there. Kissing away the tear before the next one fell. His tongue was tracing up its path. Licking away the overwhelming emotion. A gentle kiss was placed on her closed eye. Then the other. He kissed her cheeks and her nose and her forehead, and lastly her lips. Lingering there. The taste of salt on his tongue.

Then he pulled away from her, disposing of the condom before collecting her in his arms and covering their bodies in a thick duvet.

As she lay in his embrace, sated and happy, Lily wondered if she did herself a disservice by waiting so long. Could she have had this before?

'No,' she heard Julian say. 'I know what you're thinking, and it wouldn't be like this with anyone else. This is us.'

Her eyes began to droop as Julian stroked his fingers through her hair, and it wasn't long at all before Lily was sound asleep. Her last thought was that this date wasn't just for their plan. This was more. This was so much more…

The first thing Lily noticed when she woke up was the empty bed. She had woken briefly earlier, to the warmth of Julian's naked body pressing against her, his arms wrapped tightly around her. Deep steady breaths had told her he was fast asleep but now the sheets were cold where had lain.

She emerged from under the covers that were so carefully tucked around her, brushing her hair away from her face. Rubbing the sleep from her eyes, she finally looked around the room she had slept in.

The ceiling and two walls were made entirely out of panels of glass. Above her the sky was still a deep blue, slowly turning lighter. The panoramic view allowed her to see the golden rays as the sun slowly began to rise. The wall behind the headboard and the one on one side of the room were the only solid ones. There wasn't much in this room. A massive bed, two lights fixed above the nightstand, and in the corner where the three glass walls met, sat a solitary chair with a lamp arching over it.

So much space to hold so little, but it didn't need more. Didn't need art or ostentatious furniture when all she could imagine doing was sitting in bed and watching the Bay. The unmistakable bridge was silhouetted against the morning sun, slowly showing hints of that bright orange colour.

Julian had created this for himself. A little piece of heaven that he didn't invite anyone into. And she couldn't blame him. Not after what he'd said. This was obviously his refuge, and he had invited her into it.

Her heart thumping at the knowledge, Lily tried to keep her head. Moving in with him was a necessary part of their ruse. They had chemistry—that had been evident from the start—and maybe he was coming to trust her, but if last night had been such a mammoth step in whatever their relationship was, wouldn't Julian still be here this morning?

She thought back to how he had avoided her before. Was he doing the same now? Trying to push her away because he regretted saying too much? Being with her? After all it had been her first time. She had nothing to compare it to. What if it hadn't been as good for him? Not nearly as life-altering?

That was entirely possible. She was inexperienced. He might have just been leaning into their attraction. Maybe in being with her he was trying to indulge so it wouldn't be as potent any more. Would make their interactions more bearable for their plan.

The problem was that for her the lines were becoming blurred. This relationship wasn't real, but everything she had felt the night before had been. Julian had confided in her and she had given him her virginity. Those things weren't fake. So where did they go from here? Because she still wanted her freedom and Julian definitely wanted that energy deal.

Lily had to get out of this room.

But she was naked.

She stomped over to his closet, sliding the door open and stepping into a space that lit up when she walked in. Rows of suits and shirts sat neatly, evenly spaced on the rails. Ties, watches, shoes—everything perfectly displayed. Perfectly ordered.

'This is why I need control, Lily.'

This was beyond control. This was keeping himself on an impossibly tight leash.

'You make me want to lose control!'

She was chaos to him…and order and chaos were mutually exclusive. They could never have anything beyond this fake engagement.

Breathing suddenly became difficult, especially when she felt as if her heart was being split in two. She wanted more with him, but now she was faced with the evidence that it wasn't possible, and it hurt so much more than she could have imagined.

She found a neatly folded white T-shirt and slipped it over her head. It was far too long on her, but that suited her just fine.

Fully intending to go to her room, dress as quickly as possible and leave, Lily stepped into the hallway and heard a metallic clang followed by a series of other strange noises. Following them, she came to the open door of a gym, and just as she reached it Julian walked through. Shirtless and sweaty.

Her mouth dried as she looked at him. Sweatpants sitting low on his hips. Buds in his ears. His hair damp and sticking to his forehead.

Lily reached to pluck one of the buds out of his ear and placed it in her own. She wrinkled her nose at the screamed-out lyrics, the aggressive thumping beat, and placed it back into his ear. She saw his lips twitch in amusement.

She'd just about turned to go back the way she'd

come when he caught her wrist and pulled her back. The ear buds were in his hand now, which he was sliding into his pocket.

'I was hoping you would sleep in,' he said.

'I'm late. I should be at Crème already.'

Why was this so awkward?

'I'm certain you don't have to be the one to open up every day. So why don't you tell me why you're really up so early?'

'You weren't in bed. I just thought… It really doesn't matter. I should get dressed.'

'You just thought…?'

She could see he wouldn't let it go, and knew he'd probably be able to see straight through any lie. 'I know last night was different for each of us,' she said. 'It probably wasn't that enjoyable for you. But for me…'

Heat burned her face. She could only imagine how red it would be. And now, to her absolute mortification, he was trying not to smile.

'That's what you're worried about?'

He tugged her into the gym, sitting her down at the end of a padded bench and kneeling in front of her, his hands on the tops of her thighs. Lily tugged the hem of her borrowed T-shirt further down.

'Sunshine, last night was beyond words. I could have you every day in every way and it still wouldn't be enough. I'm greedy for you. And leaving you asleep in that bed this morning, not waking you with my tongue and my fingers, took more strength than I knew I possessed.'

Lily opened her mouth but no words came out. Not when his words had her growing moist.

'My leaving that bed had nothing to do with how

much last night meant, or how much I want you, and everything to do with who I am.'

'What do you mean?' Lily asked softly.

'I'm awake before sunrise every day so I can do this.' He gestured around the gym. 'So that I can be at my best for every moment of my day. For IRES.'

'You work every day?' But Lily already knew the answer to that, even without his solemn nod. 'Julian, that isn't sustainable.'

'It is for me. It's what I do. No matter where I am.'

'Why do you work so hard?'

'IRES is all I have. For what was sacrificed…' Julian shook his head '…it has to mean something. I need IRES to be a success. It makes me worth something.'

'You already are.' She cupped his cheek. 'You can't just work. You need to relax too. Do something you enjoy.'

'I do.'

Lily didn't believe him, but she asked anyway. 'What's that?'

'Krav Maga.'

'Krav…? Julian, that doesn't count!'

She realised how lucky Lincoln had been to leave Crème unscathed.

'Would it make you happy if did something different?' he asked, and there was a spark of mischief in his eyes.

'Maybe…'

He gave her a wicked grin and pushed her down onto the bench, bunching the T-shirt shirt at her waist and lowering his mouth to her sex.

Before all thought could be pushed out of her head she held on to the new goal she had. To help Julian really live his life.

* * *

They were well and truly late now, but Julian didn't care. Not when his lips were sliding against Lily's as steaming water rained down on them in his cavernous shower. Holding her back to his chest, he slid his fingers in and out of her, heard her moans echoing off the tiles until she loudly came apart for him.

Then he lathered and soaped her, bringing her to the edge and leaving her there.

'A promise for later,' he whispered in her ear.

Seeing her in his T-shirt had punched such a wave of possessiveness through him he'd very nearly told her that was all she must wear in his home. But somehow he had managed not to act like a neanderthal when she'd sought reassurance.

Julian couldn't believe Lily had thought he hadn't enjoyed himself. He was certain sex would never be the same for him again. It certainly wouldn't be after she'd left his life—and she did have to leave. He still couldn't give himself over to love, or whatever this was.

Stepping out of the shower, he wrapped a towel around his waist before picking up his razor in the routine he had performed every morning since leaving his stepfather's house. Work out, shower, shave, work hard for as long as it took to achieve his day's goal—and repeat it all the next day. It had served him well. But now he wanted more than that.

His gaze flicked to Lily in the mirror. He wasn't worthy of her. He would lose her. It was inevitable. Everyone left. By choice or not—it was immaterial. His father had died before he'd had a chance to know him, his mother had lived a tortured life before she died, and Lily would leave because all she was looking for was her freedom.

So he was faced with his own choice: he could push her away or he could enjoy this while it lasted.

So, no choice at all then. Because he craved her like air.

'Arum is hosting the Zenith dinner the day after tomorrow,' Lily said while drying her hair.

Zenith was the exclusive network started by the old money families of San Francisco. Julian still hadn't received his invitation, and this would be the first test to see if he was making any impression with this plan that they had embarked on.

'I know,' he replied.

'You know you're my plus one, right? Even if you don't get an invitation, you'll still attend.'

'I know that, but getting one will make convincing those people to work with me much simpler.'

'You still have time,' Lily offered.

He did, but it wasn't all that much. The longer it took for him to be accepted into the ranks of this group, the further away the Arum deal would get.

CHAPTER ELEVEN

THE INVITATION LANDED on Julian's desk that very same afternoon.

Step one was complete.

Now he would have to gauge how his relationship with Lily affected Zenith's perception of him.

But for the first time since coming up with this plan, Julian was unhappy. Something between him and Lily had shifted. He no longer wanted to flaunt their relationship in the faces of those who wouldn't accept him without her. He wanted to protect what they had behind very thick walls. Except it wasn't just up to him. Lily would benefit too, and any change in the plan would affect her life. She had given him no indication that her wishes had changed and he couldn't expect them to—especially when all he could commit to was something temporary. His goals hadn't changed either.

So he would continue with his end of the bargain and when Arum signed it would all be worth it.

He hoped.

Julian up picked the invitation card, eyeing the Zenith logo. These people advertised their power and wealth unapologetically. It was ridiculous to him that he could create an international powerhouse and still have to cater to their whims to get a real foothold in his own city. But he had to. Because not achieving this goal meant failure, and he couldn't withstand that.

While it irritated him, it wouldn't have bothered him as much before. Now it felt like the price was growing. And that price was his relationship with Lily. Yet everything rested on this event. His future and the future of IRES.

What he needed was time with Lily away from all this. Time that was just theirs.

Julian had Lily pressed against his side in the back of the car. He noticed her fingers tracing along the stones of the elaborate yellow diamond choker he had given her before they'd left the house.

They were both clad in black, as per the invitation, but for some reason he'd hated the idea of Lily in something so lifeless, so he'd presented her with a gift. A little bit of the colour that he had grown so accustomed to seeing her in.

She was staring out of the window, but he knew she was looking at nothing in particular.

Raising the partition between them and his driver, Julian pressed a kiss to her temple. 'Don't be nervous. I'm not letting you out of my sight.'

She leaned into him with a sigh, but said nothing, and Julian suddenly wished they were anywhere but here.

But he couldn't take his eyes off the goal.

For either of them.

They approached a magnificent high-end hotel, recognisable immediately by its carved façade and towering stone pillars and a landmark in San Francisco. It was fitting that the dinner should be held here, where business had been conducted by the wealthy and influential for over a hundred years.

Julian himself had used their boardroom facilities to secure several deals. It seemed like a sign.

The car pulled up to the entrance and once the door was opened for him Julian stepped out and offered his hand to Lily.

Every head looked their way when they entered the room. Everyone saw her hold on to Julian's hand. Watched as she stepped even closer to his side.

He leaned down to whisper in her ear. 'Are you ready for this?'

'Funny, I was just about to ask you the same thing.'

Lily smiled. She could have fooled anyone else here, he thought, but not him. He could see she was nervous about being here. Facing the repercussions of their actions. But he also knew she would do anything to have her life back, and with or without him she would handle these people with grace.

'Here comes our first test,' Julian said, watching Devan approach with an impassive look on his face. 'Shah.' He held out his hand.

'Ford,' Devan greeted him, taking it.

Julian's eyes never once left his and he noticed a shift there. Instead of outright animosity there was just caution. He looked at his sister and kissed her cheek.

'How are you, Lily?'

'Happy.'

She beamed, and Devan clearly believed it, because his shoulders sagged. With relief or resignation Julian didn't know, but it was a start.

'Good. That's good,' Devan said quietly.

There was a hint of sadness in his tone that irked Julian.

'The house isn't quite the same without you,' he went on.

'You're going to have to get used to that, Dev,' she told him.

Lily smiled up at Julian and he felt a fist clench around his heart. He kissed her temple without thinking. A small smile broke through his features without his permission.

Devan noticed. Everyone did.

'Would you like a drink?' Julian asked her, offering Lily a moment alone with her brother.

'Yes, please.'

Except she didn't let go of him. Chose to remain by his side instead of her brother's. He wasn't prepared for how that felt...

'Ford, wait,' Devan said as the two of them turned away. 'I want to talk to you.'

'About...?'

'The energy deal.'

Julian tensed. Then he pivoted to face Devan.

'You want in, and I'm prepared to help you. Under one condition.'

'What's that?'

'You make Lily happy. I know you can keep her safe, and I thank you for doing so, but if I find out that you've used her, not only will you not get the deal, I'll see to it no one in San Francisco works with you again.'

'Dev!' Lily reprimanded.

'Easily done.'

Julian extended his hand and Devan shook it firmly.

They stepped towards the bar, but didn't make it very far before they were swallowed up by a group of people. Julian already knew every single one of them, but still he stood there through the introductions, shaking hands and paying compliments.

These were the people he needed on his side. The shareholders of Arum.

'Congratulations on your engagement!' gushed an older woman covered in glittering diamonds. 'Can I see the ring?'

Julian wrapped an arm around Lily's waist, fusing her to his side as she held out her left hand.

'Oh, that's beautiful!'

'Julian chose it.'

Lily was the very definition of a charming fiancée. He remembered what a terrible liar she was, so seeing her so effortlessly playing the part should be worrying him. Except he realised that when it came to Lily his walls had come crashing down, and he wanted every bit of affection she had it in her to give.

'He has great taste.'

'Clearly.'

Julian looked down at her with softness in his heart.

'I have to say, Ford, I was rather surprised to hear about your engagement. I think we all were,' said a greying man in a sharp suit.

'Some things aren't for the world to see,' Julian replied easily.

Whatever this was budding between them, it was theirs alone.

'I couldn't agree more,' the man said with a twinkling smile. 'I saw you having a chat with Devan?'

'He is Lily's brother.'

Julian would give nothing away. He wanted to know where they stood before he said anything.

'Yes, but you must know how the shareholding in Arum is. If you can convince Devan to vote in your favour, we may be inclined to do the same.' The man handed Julian a business card. 'Give me a call. I expect to see a lot more of you at these events, Ford.'

It was music to his ears.

When they finally made it to the bar Julian placed their order then pulled Lily aside. He had been so attentive all evening, she thought. He could clearly see that she was apprehensive about seeing Lincoln again. Not that she anticipated him making a scene—he never would—but he had been so angry the last time she'd seen him.

She felt warm fingers brush against her cheek, followed by soft lips on hers. Julian's tongue caressed hers sweetly, his kiss obliterating the worry from her mind.

'We should be mingling,' Lily said softly.

Julian's breath kissed her ear, sending tingles right through her.

'I don't really care about that. I just want to take you back home, lay you out and feast on you until you're breathless and panting my name.'

It took every ounce of self-control she had not to moan right there. The self-satisfied smirk on his face told her he knew exactly what he was doing. She would have dragged him away herself if she hadn't understood how important this night was.

'Well, you're just going to have to wait.'

'Am I?'

Julian pulled her body flush against his. Powerful

thighs pressed against hers. His manhood and his muscular torso.

'Yes.'

He was making it very hard for her to think clearly. Especially because he was allowing her to see his playful side. This man who didn't smile or laugh did so freely around her, and he was doing so now, in the presence of others. And they noticed.

How could they not when his hands had been all over her all night? Every touch sending shockwaves to her core.

'Lily… Ford.'

The chilly voice made the smile drop off her face. She felt Julian put his arm around her shoulders as they both turned to face Lincoln.

'Hi, Linc,' she greeted him.

He said nothing. Blue eyes boring into hers.

'Harrison.' She heard Julian say.

'I suppose congratulations are in order,' he said stiffly.

'Thank you.'

He was only doing this to keep up appearances, because a Harrison very clearly giving a Shah the cold shoulder would set tongues wagging. And they couldn't have that.

'The board can't stop talking about you two. Seems like you're a changed man, Ford.'

'I'm the same man. Lily just brings out a different side of me.'

Flashes of that night in the pagoda came to her mind. Of being in his bed for the first time. Of him giving her the necklace she wore. All the hidden pieces of himself he'd shown her. They were always there. No one else cared to see it, and Lily couldn't think of a greater travesty, but it made what they had all the more special.

Lincoln was looking at her again. Something wavered in his gaze. The look of someone having lost a prize. She hated it.

Julian must have noticed the change in her, because he excused them, leading the way to the tables that were now filling up before dinner was presented.

And that was when she met Henry Cross.

Of course she knew of him, and had wondered what he would be like since the first time Julian had mentioned him, but she hadn't expected to meet him here.

'I'm glad you made it, Julian,' Henry said. 'And you must be Lily. Pleasure to finally meet you.'

'And you.'

Lily smiled politely. The tables were filling quickly, and she noted that everyone around them was from Arum. Her brother was seated opposite her, looking uncomfortable next to Lincoln, but Julian wouldn't let her focus on that.

Throughout their meal, and through all the chatter, she relished the touch of his thumb on the back of her neck. The whispers and the kisses. All of it distracting her from the fact she was sharing a table with the people she was hoping to get away from. The very people Julian was trying to win over.

The feeling she'd had when she'd walked into his closet swarmed over her. She wanted him so much, but this could never last. Not when they had such opposing goals.

When the meal was done and most of the seats vacated, Henry asked Lily to stay.

'You can go, Julian. You have work to do.'

Lily watched with shock as Julian rolled his eyes and then obeyed and stood. He kissed her cheek and turned to his mentor.

'Don't steal my date,' Julian warned, before walking away.

Lily wanted to burst out laughing. She hadn't thought there was a soul on earth that Julian would listen to. But maybe it was more that Henry understood what Julian needed, and in turn Julian had shown her how much he trusted Henry.

'I have not seen him this happy in my life. You've done this, Lily,' said Henry, as he watched Julian walk away.

'Thank you.'

Lily's heart squeezed at the tenderness in his kind brown eyes. 'You care for Julian a lot.'

'I don't know if he's told you how we met?'

'Not much.'

Lily was on tenterhooks. Eager to collect every little piece of Julian she could.

'I went to give a talk at his college. I could tell there was something special about him, and when we spoke I saw a young man with a massive intellect in worn-down thrift store clothes. I knew then I couldn't let him languish, just because he didn't have the privilege of his fellows. So I took him under my wing. He was so serious. Never smiled. Not even on the day of his graduation.'

'You were there?' Lily was so glad that Julian had found someone to care for him.

'I was. I taught him everything I knew about business, but it became clear very quickly that he saw things differently, and soon the young upstart was giving me advice.' Henry laughed with clear affection. 'But I didn't want him working for me.'

'You didn't?' Lily asked, confused. Henry seemed to love Julian so much, and it seemed rather strange that he hadn't wanted to give him a place in his company.

'No. No doubt he would have made me a great deal of money, but with everything that young man had been through he needed someone to support his dreams.'

'How did you do that?' she asked.

'He gave me the capital to start IRES.'

Lily started at Julian's voice.

He sat elegantly in the chair beside hers.

Henry chuckled. 'He's like a son to me.'

'You're growing sentimental, old man.'

He seemed unbothered by Henry revealing so much of his past.

'Maybe I am.'

Lily loved the fact that she was being allowed to witness the special relationship they had with each other. Loved it that Henry had never been put off by Julian's coldness. He just accepted him.

'When I found out about this engagement I will admit I was concerned, but you've done well, Julian.'

'I have.' Julian's fingers curled around hers. 'We should go…'

All three rose from their chairs and Henry leaned in close to Lily. 'I'll be grateful to you for ever. If you ever need anything at all, you need only ask.'

He gave her a peck on the cheek and placed his card in her hand, then he shook Julian's and left.

CHAPTER TWELVE

'THAT WENT WELL,' Lily said, once they were settled in the back seat of the car.

It had gone far better than either of them had anticipated. All Julian had to do now was solidify the relationship with Devan and the shareholders were his. Yet that was far from the reason tonight had been so momentous.

Henry had told Lily things that Julian often wished his mentor would forget, but he wasn't upset. He wanted her to know him. On some level he understood that even when she eventually walked away, a little piece of him would be tucked away with her and it would be safe.

He pulled her across his lap, kissing her neck, holding her as she melted against him, wanting so desperately to make her happy.

'I have a surprise for you,' she said breathlessly.

'For me?'

'Yes, but before I can tell you what it is, I need to know if you trust me.'

'Of course I do.' Trust wasn't something Julian often did, but he trusted Lily. Trusted her with his past, his plans…

'I want to take you away,' she said.

'Where to?' he said against her neck, trailing his fingers slowly up her leg.

'Paris. I've made arrangements for Crème. All you have to do is say the word.'

'Paris?' He stopped his hand on the inside of her thigh, felt her tremble.

She touched his forehead to his. 'Come to France with me.'

'Of course I will.'

Hadn't he been wishing for time alone with her? She was giving him exactly what he wanted.

'We can take my jet.'

He saw relief flood through her and trailed his hand further. The damp fabric between her thighs kissed his fingers and he groaned, eyes burning into hers.

'You've kissed me and touched me and teased me. And I've been aching for you all night,' she told him.

Julian's lips swooped down on hers in a fiery kiss that had him growing hard in an instant, cursing the fact that they were in this car that would be arriving at his home within minutes.

They broke apart and without a moment's pause he had his phone to his ear, issuing quick commands.

'We're going to have to wait, Sunshine. Give me an hour and I'll make it up to you.'

As promised, in an hour they were buckled into plush cream seats on Julian's jet and taxiing down the runway. Julian sat opposite her, with a table between them, making no move to touch her. Though his face remained neutral, there was a glint in his eye, and Lily knew then that he wasn't breaking his promise…he was just making her want him even more without laying a finger on her.

Finally he grinned, covering it up with a large hand as he looked out of the window.

San Francisco was a web of golden light as they lifted into the sky. No sign of the steep roads and iconic houses. Up here she could find no reason to be anxious, no anger towards her family. Those were all problems left on the ground.

Lily hadn't felt this serene in all the years since she had returned from France. But now it was as if a heavy cloak had been cast off and she was free. She wanted to help Julian live, and Paris did just that for her. This way she could take him away from everything that weighed on his shoulders, from that maddening discipline, and help him relax.

In the back of the car she had seen the understanding in his face when she'd invited him on this trip. He appreciated how much it would mean to her, and she wanted to share this part of herself with this man who was not going to be around for much longer, if tonight was anything to go by. Because once Devan and the board voted to sign with IRES, Lincoln would too. He wouldn't vote against his partner.

The smart thing to do would be to distance herself from Julian. She was already too close. She wanted him so badly. But he had never once said that he was considering any kind of future with her.

Even after he'd told her about his stepfather, he'd said he couldn't let anyone in. But maybe it was time for him to let go of the fear of what he might turn into. Maybe she could show him who he really was.

Would he let her?

The plane levelled off and drinks were served. A short glass of something red, diffused slowly into clear liquid. The glass, frosted with condensation, sat on a coaster and she reached to stir it with the black straw before taking a sip. She didn't bother asking what it was. It refreshed her and that was all that mattered.

'Tired?' Julian asked.

'I'm fine,' she said. But when she leaned her head back she could feel the tendrils of sleep creeping over her.

She felt him undoing her seat belt and carrying her to the back of the plane. She should have protested, but it was comfortable in his arms, warm and safe, so Lily let him carry her to the bed and drape the sheets over her. But she wouldn't let him leave.

'Stay.'

She held her breath while he watched her. For a second? A minute? A pause in time. Then he took off his shoes and jacket and slid between the sheets, pulling her to him. She went willingly into his arms.

'You should sleep. I'll be right here when you wake.'

'Kiss me, please.'

He didn't hesitate. Not for a moment.

This kiss was soft, gentle. Sweet beyond imagining. It didn't ignite her, like his lips usually did. No... It melted her. Stirred her slowly. His fingers combing through her hair had her sighing into his mouth. But before she was ready to stop his lips were gone, pressing a kiss to her forehead.

His fingertips stroked lazily back and forth on her scalp, lulling Lily to sleep. She thought she heard him speak, but she was too far under a thick cloud of sleep to parse his words.

* * *

Only once they had begun their descent did Julian rouse Lily. After landing there was a blur of activity, and soon the two of them were in an electric sports car that Julian drove through the streets with such ease Lily wondered just how familiar he already was with Paris.

That question was soon answered when they reached a beautiful old building in the Seventh Arrondissement. They went up to the very top floor and she watched Julian pull out a key to unlock a door, which he held open for her.

'Welcome home.' He smiled.

'Home? You own this place?' she asked, stepping into a light foyer with wooden herringbone floors and large windows.

'Yes. I have properties all over the world.'

Of course he did. She should have considered it before. But when they'd been in his house she hadn't been able to picture him anywhere else.

He slipped his hands into his pockets. 'Why don't you take a look out of the window?'

Lily gasped. She felt as if she could touch the Eiffel Tower if she stuck her hand out far enough. Just a handful of trees separated them from the breathtaking landmark.

'You have a beautiful home.'

It really was. A beautiful blend of modern and classical French design.

She felt his arms wrap around her. 'Come on, we've still got plenty of light left in the day. We're going out.'

His bedroom was just as exquisite as the rest of the apartment. After a quick shower Lily dressed in a flowing skirt and light jacket. She was just draping her bag across her body when Julian stepped out of his walk-in closet.

She was at a loss for words.

This was what he looked like when he relaxed.

There was just a hint of stubble on his face, long, powerful legs were sheathed in light denim, and a white T-shirt stretched across his chest. The gold ring that pierced his ear was twinkling, as if it held the secret of Julian's transformation.

It took nothing away from him. This Julian still had that air of danger his suits advertised so flawlessly, except now he looked more human somehow. Not the man who had to shave every say, who had to only wear those suits and workout at precisely the same time each morning because he had to be—had to be—so perfectly disciplined for every moment of his life.

'Ready to go?'

No, she wasn't. She didn't want to leave this apartment at all now. Didn't want to waste a single moment of this Julian when she knew he would disappear the moment they went back to San Francisco.

'Where are we going?' Lily asked.

Maybe she could convince him to make it a short outing…

'Where do you want to go?'

Her very first thought was the pavement café that held so many great memories. And so that was where they went.

Sitting outside at a wrought-iron table, they were nothing more than a couple having coffee. The Arum deal, Lincoln and Devan all seemed like faraway concerns that couldn't touch them here.

'Sunshine,' Julian said as she reached the end of telling him the story of something that had happened at the café. 'It's okay to come back here because it brings you happiness, but you can't use it to escape to the past. Look forward. You need to create new memories.'

He was right—she did. And she would. With him. Those were the only new memories she really wanted, but she was too afraid to say that. Afraid to break the spell. Because he still hadn't said that they were done with faking. That this was real. She wanted to believe that it was. It *felt* real.

'The future seems a little uncertain right now,' she admitted.

'It always will—but you make a plan and you stick to it and all the pieces will fall into place.'

Would one of those pieces be him?

In those days spent in Paris, creating new memories was exactly what they did. Lily took Julian to all the places she wanted to share with only him, and he did the same for her. They'd be driving for hours, only to realise that they would rather be holed up in his apartment.

On their second day she learned that his French was perfectly fluent and cringed at the thought of her teasing when he'd taken her to that play.

Every single day was perfect. There wasn't a camera to be found, and that allowed them to carve out precious moments for themselves.

One moment was made all the more special as Lily stood alone in the Hall of Mirrors at the Palace of Versailles. Bright sunlight poured in through the large windows, reflecting off every sparkling surface. The golden statues were nearly glowing. Above were chandeliers so breathtakingly intricate she couldn't stop looking at them. And the ceiling… It was beauty beyond words.

Julian had managed to arrange a private tour, just for them. Another memory made with him for her to pocket away.

She glanced sidelong at him as he studied a statue of a golden woman bearing a crystal lamp. This man had brought her here, showed him a piece of himself and made her happy. Simply looking at him made her heart race.

'What's on your mind?' he asked, turning to her.

'Nothing,' she lied. When he cocked his eyebrow, she chuckled. 'It's just unfair how you affect me.'

'You think it's not the same for me?'

Julian was incredulous. How could she not see what she did to him?

'Come with me.'

He was going to set the record straight. He was in France with her because she had asked him to come, but still she thought he wasn't completely under her spell.

It was ridiculous.

He took her hand and led her through the palace and the magnificent gardens to the hotel in the palace grounds. They entered a grand apartment with its gilded walls decorated similarly to the palace that could be viewed from the window.

Julian had booked it for complete privacy but he did not stop until they were in the largest suite allowing her to walk a few steps away from him. She pivoted on the spot, watching him. He knew she would be reading clear want on his face. This was how he would show her exactly what she made him feel.

'Take off your clothes and get on the bed.'

Lily cocked a brow at his command, but he knew she would obey. It was written in the way her eyes grew heavy, in the breaths that seemed to come a little more raggedly, and the blush creeping up her neck. Julian watched, cataloguing every minute detail, every change in her body.

She drew her shirt over her head, letting it slip through the tips of her fingers to the floor.

Julian stood still. Trying with all his might to control the want ravaging him. Trying not to cross the distance between them and take her in his arms. He couldn't do that. He had to show her what he couldn't say. What he might never be able to say. Even though the words had been dancing around his mind constantly.

'I love you.'

They had been the last words he had said to his mother at her bedside. The last time he had said them at all. There was no way he would ever be able to say them again.

Julian pulled his own shirt over his head and threw it to one side. Lily paused her movement, her gaze raking over his body, and he could have sworn he felt it like a touch. Drawing the corner of her lip between her teeth, she removed the rest of her clothing, with Julian just a step behind.

Then she climbed into the centre of the large, four-poster canopied bed and leaned back against the pillows.

'Touch yourself,' he said, hoarse.

Her skin flamed, and he could see her swallow hard, but despite her shyness Lily raised a hand and trailed it down her stomach. Teasing.

As hard as he was, he knew it wasn't just arousal

that coursed through him, but pride. He was so proud
of this woman who didn't back down from any challenge. She just reached within herself and pulled from
her limitless reserves of strength.

So he would make her invincible. No one was ever
going to try to control her again. She wouldn't be shy
about her pleasure, wouldn't worry about her freedom,
nor care if anyone was there to support her. Because
he would make sure she knew she needed no one. The
world should be bowing to her, begging to be allowed
into her universe.

And even though he couldn't say the words playing
in his mind, Julian knew that he loved her. It was an
absolute, immutable truth. Even though he'd tried to
fight it. Even though he knew what love could do to a
person. Even though he knew this couldn't be for ever.
Julian had fallen in love with her.

He watched her fingers slide lazily over her sex,
heard a gasp escaping her at her own touch, and with
eyes locked on hers he grasped his hardness, matching
her slow, languid pace.

The muscles in his abdomen tensed, pleading with
him to go faster, but he wouldn't. He leaned against
the wall behind him. The cool surface was welcome
against his heated skin. Lily was flushed, her breathing
growing more uneven the longer she watched him. And
as her fingers moved faster, so did his hand. A moan
came from both of them, the two sounds intertwining
in the quiet room.

'Lily…' he rasped. An invocation.

Through the haze, he could see understanding light
her eyes. She slowed her hand right down and so did

he. His obedience to her order was unwavering, making him groan…a rough, strangled sound.

A feline smirk curved her lips. She controlled him. Controlled his very pleasure. Her eyes sparkled with an excitement that made his pulse hammer even harder. She pushed up on her elbows, a look of challenge in her eyes, and it was the sexiest thing he had ever witnessed to see Lily come into her power.

She'd taken a wrecking ball to his high walls, exposing him. All of him. Raw and unguarded. She saw his smiles and laughter. His ability to joke and be playful. Not because he'd let her, but because there was no other way he could exist around her.

Lily had become his safe space. And, to his immense surprise, he didn't hate it. There was a settling in him almost like peace, knowing she saw him. Maybe not the brutal truth of him—not yet—but he would hide nothing from her now.

Nothing except those three words he would never utter.

Julian's muscles tensed and bunched. His shoulders chorded as she toyed with that control. Her breasts were heaving just as much as he struggled for his next breath. But he would say nothing. He would revel in all that she did to him.

He could tell the game was becoming too much for her, that she was on the verge of losing control, and she closed her eyes, throwing her head back on the soft down pillow.

'No, keep your eyes open,' Julian instructed in a low, tight voice. 'See what you do to me.'

And she did. That obsidian gaze never wavered as her fingers slipped between her folds, faster and faster. Julian could feel the coiling beginning at the base of his spine. And then Lily was calling out his name as she shattered on the bed.

Her fingers stilled.

'Keep going. Don't stop.'

Despite her writhing and mewling she listened to him. He knew how sensitive she would be, but she listened because he had power over her too. Her fingers moved as quickly as his hand, and then he felt his entire body go taut as his release burst from him, clouding his vision and stealing his breath…his strength.

Julian dropped his head against the wall, needing a moment before he was able to prowl to the bed, climb over her. One hand held him up while the other slid over her smooth skin. Over her thighs and her ribs and her breast.

His fingers wrapped around her neck as he indulged them in a firm but gentle kiss. His lips blazed a trail to the base of her throat. Slowly, so slowly, kissing their way up her neck, his lips brushing her ear.

'Now do you see what you do to me?' he whispered. 'You hold me in the palm of your hand, Sunshine.'

'Julian…'

She breathed hard against his neck. A tremor went through him.

'You do that to me too.'

He scooped her against him, rolling onto his back and holding her tightly. She settled with her head on his chest. There was an end point looming, so Julian was determined to savour this with Lily while he could—because he was certain he would never experience it again.

Legs entwined with his, her arm draped over his rippling stomach, Lily trailed her fingers over the pattern of the tree inked into his side. She smiled as his skin pebbled from her light touch, but he made no move to stop her.

She drew over the black lines. 'Was it painful?'

'Yes.' His voice was soft.

'When did you get it done?'

Her voice was as soft as his as her finger followed the line of a dead branch reaching towards his nipple.

'While I was at college.'

After he'd left his stepfather's house.

'After I met Henry and he showed me what it meant to own a company. Understanding the dynamics was easy, and I let myself believe in a future where I had all the power.'

Despite his quiet, even voice, Lily could feel how his heart sped up. Hazarding a look at his face, she saw that he was looking out of the window. Who knew what he saw? But that sadness she often caught a glimpse of seemed to be leaking out of him now, and she had to turn away lest she dissolve into tears and this wasn't about her needing comfort.

'Before that I was still convinced I just had to survive. It was all I was used to...'

Lily had to shove aside the burning anger clawing at her throat. He shouldn't have had to be used to that. How was it fair that Julian had had to deal with the aftermath of abuse and his stepfather had paid no price?

'But once I saw what I could achieve I just looked forward.'

'And that's when you had this done?'

'Yes.'

She looked again at the knotted bark and gnarled roots. The stunning leaves were hidden from her right now, but she refused to move from her position. She could guess the meaning of the tattoo now. To grow from something dead, something just trying to remain anchored into something that flourished. That triumphed. He'd survived his abuse, but when she thought about how disciplined he was, how he never wanted to lose control, she knew he hadn't healed. He was still running from it. From that life.

'And this one?' she asked, running her fingers over the numbers on his chest to keep him talking.

He was silent for a moment. She looked up to see his eyes were closed.

'My mother's birthday.'

Her heart crumbled at the raw pain in his whispered words. The long string of roman numerals stood out boldly against his smooth, light skin. She pressed a kiss to it, then another. His fingers sank into her hair, their gentle touch only fuelling her anger further. Her devastation on his behalf.

It was a long while before she could trust herself to speak without her voice trembling. 'What was she like?'

Something told Lily that, while he carried a constant reminder of her, Julian didn't let himself think of his mother very often—and he needed to. She wanted to help him while he was being this open with her, because she had no idea when he would clam up. Which question would be one too many. When he would decide this was much too real for their arrangement and push her away.

The idea that he would was like a knife in her chest...

'Alice Sullivan was...'

Sullivan? Lily thought. Probably his stepfather's name.

'She was wonderful. When it was just us two, she

was happy and bubbly. Everyone loved her. But the more conspicuous her bruises became, the less she would go out or interact with anyone. Slowly that light died…but she still loved him.'

Lily tightened her arms around him.

'Did you ever wish for things to be different? For your mother to have left?'

'Yes.' Julian answered. 'I quickly realised that while she loved me, she couldn't choose me. Nothing will change that.'

Lily's heart broke. Julian was still angry—she knew that much. He had accepted what had happened but he hadn't moved on. No matter what he said. Because if he had, he would have love and a family. Friends beyond Henry.

'She was as protective as she could be,' he said. 'But I don't think she was terribly brave.'

No, because 'brave' to a little boy would mean a mother who would have picked him up and left that house. She must have been broken too if she'd thought she couldn't leave. No one was at fault here except Julian's stepfather.

Lily could only imagine what that must have done to Julian. For him to know every day that his mother couldn't choose him. To know that he was too young or too weak to protect her, even though he'd tried.

He was quiet for a long time before he added, 'It was my fault.'

'What was?'

Her heart had almost stopped beating. Surely he couldn't think he was to blame for what they had been through.

'Her death. The abuse.'

'No,' Lily said firmly.

'I could have found the money for my mother's treatment…stood up to him sooner. I was capable. And I enjoyed putting him on his ass.' Julian smiled but it was more a baring of teeth. 'But I was filled with so much hate that I didn't realise I could do it until it was too late.'

'Julian…' Her voice was strangled.

'Was?' He laughed out the word. 'I still am full of hate.'

And Lily heard it then. Hate. Not just for his stepfather, but himself too.

'That's not true.'

'You think I didn't already have the idea for my invention when she got sick? I did nothing with it. I could have sold it and got us the hell out of there. But I did nothing. I held on to it until it could make me money and the cost, Lily, was my mother's life. That's why I need unparalleled success for IRES. I sacrificed my mother, and I need that loss to mean something.'

'You were just a child, Julian. You can't take that on yourself. You were surviving as best you could.' Silent tears trickled down Lily's cheeks. His voice was so lifeless. Hollow.

'That first time he beat her was after they got into an argument over me.'

Lily stopped breathing. She was certain he had never said those words to anyone before. Wondered how often he had dwelled on it. So much heartache. It wasn't fair for one person to carry this much.

She shifted on the bed, nuzzling his ear with her nose, and was rewarded with the smallest of smiles. 'It wasn't your fault—you hear me?' she said adamantly.

She would keep saying it until he believed it. Even when whatever they were to each other came to an end.

He didn't respond.

They were quiet for a long time. She would have thought him asleep had it not been for his fingers, rubbing lazy circles on her skin.

'And this?' She touched the gold ring in his helix, hoping he would keep talking.

That got a bigger smile out of Julian. 'A little bit of rebellion,' he said.

'Oh?'

'I quickly learnt the best way to avoid my stepfather was not to be at home, so as soon as I had grown enough I got a job after school, working at a tattoo and piercing shop. I was underage, but I was tall and sufficiently well-built enough to pass for older, and they paid me in cash. I saved every penny for my escape. Whether it was going to be through college or another way, I was determined to get out.'

'But you held on until the scholarship came through?'

'I did. I knew it would be the most permanent way to leave, and besides, I was due to graduate early.'

'So when did you get the piercing?'

'Shortly after my mother died. I knew *he* would hate it. I wouldn't have dared before then…'

'In case he took it out on her.' Lily finished for him.

Julian nodded. 'I wanted him to dare him to do something about it, but by that point he could do nothing against me. The shop used to get some really rough types coming through, so they taught me how to fight enough to make anyone think twice about causing trouble. They didn't realise that they were helping me with my stepfather too.'

His jaw clenched and a look of utter desolation crossed his face. Whatever thought he'd just had, it was obviously agonising.

'I like it,' she said.

'You do, do you?'

'Yes, but I have been wondering...'

'Why don't I just take it out and fit in?'

There he went—reading her mind again. 'Yes.'

'I don't want to fit in, Lily. This little thing—' he flicked the earring '—is a constant reminder of where I came from.'

Lily understood then. The suits were his armour, but they covered up his reminders. The earring, though, was unmissable. Any time he caught his reflection he would be reminded of who and what he was. So would everyone who encountered him. He wasn't part of their world. He wasn't spoilt and entitled. He hadn't been raised with privilege. Julian had fought. He'd fought for everything he had. Earned it.

His reputation said 'ruthless', but his appearance told every one of those Zenith businessmen that he was something different. Dangerous. Because he could surpass them even having come from nothing.

Lily kissed his jaw, and when he turned to look at her she kissed him with all the passion he brought out in her. Trying to be a balm for his soul. Wanted to tell him she accepted him. But she didn't know how he would react to that, so instead she kept kissing him. Gliding her tongue along his. Enjoying the sounds he made as he pressed their bodies together.

He needed to be broken out of his cage, and after all that he'd told her she was adamant that she would be the one to do it. Not because he needed fixing, but because he deserved to live a life free of the weight he carried.

And if anyone understood how much freedom meant, it was her.

CHAPTER THIRTEEN

BUCKLED AGAIN INTO the cream leather seat, Lily caught up on the news on Julian's tablet. After reading through article after article, she finally reached the society section.

A headline caught her attention and she froze.

Heart racing, she opened the article and began reading.

'What is it?' she heard Julian ask.

But she couldn't form a response. Not even when he came over to read over her shoulder.

On the screen, in a big close-up photo, was Lincoln with a tall blonde on his arm. Lily recognised her face. She was the daughter of one of her father's business associates, who obviously would have been one of Arthur's too.

There were several pictures, all taken on different days while Lily and Julian had been in France. The article stated that they were in a committed relationship. Lily didn't care if that was true or not, because now everyone would know that she and Lincoln were not in any way expected to be together and he had very clearly moved on.

'How does it feel to be a free woman?' asked Julian.

'I don't know…' She laughed nervously. Her family no longer controlled her destiny. It no longer mattered that she couldn't trust them, that they didn't protect her. 'I'm just hoping I'm not dreaming.'

'You're not, Sunshine.'

She was free. Really, truly free. She could live her life as she wanted to now. There was nothing holding her back. And it was all thanks to the man beside her. The one who had liberated her.

'Thank you, Julian. I'll never be able to say it enough.'

'You never have to at all.'

When she looked up at him she saw he had the strangest expression. Pleasant, but closed off. Was it because part of their agreement had come to an end? She was more than willing to help him still, and it wasn't just because that was the deal.

She wanted him to get the Arum contract because she knew that he was the best at what he did. That he cared. She wanted the old money businessmen to accept him because of who he was. To her, he was perfect. It didn't matter what he thought of this arrangement any more, because what they'd shared in France had been the most real thing she had ever experienced. It had for him too. If he needed time to see that she would give it to him, but she wasn't going to let him think that she was willing to leave.

Getting off her seat, she stood before him, curling her fingers in the lapels of his jacket. 'I am grateful, Julian, but Lincoln doesn't matter. None of them do.'

Not any more. Not when she felt so deeply for the man in front of her.

'What *does* matter?'

There was an apprehension in his eyes that he either couldn't mask or didn't bother to. Lily hoped it was the latter.

'This.'

She placed a soft kiss on his lips that had the strong bands of his arms wrapping around her. He took her with him as he sat down, on his lap, with her arms around his neck and their lips connected, and that was where she stayed for the rest of the flight.

The sun was only just going down when they returned home. And the fact that Lily now considered this house 'home' was testament to her growing feelings for Julian.

Not wanting to say goodbye to this time they had to themselves just yet, they spent most of the afternoon in bed, tangled in the soft sheets. But despite this she could see that whatever had been bothering Julian on the plane had not gone away.

She wanted to help him, but even though he had opened up to her, she didn't think he would tell her what was wrong now. She had been trying to process everything he'd told her in that bedroom. It crushed her that he blamed himself. That part of him hated himself.

He needed to come to terms with the abuse. See that none of it was his fault. Maybe then he could finally start healing. He deserved that. Deserved peace and love and acceptance.

And Lily wanted to be the one to give him those things.

Love…

She knew she was falling for him. Had known it for a while. But it had been on that plane, when she'd seen the picture of Lincoln and her first thought had been of Julian, that she'd known it was love. But he hadn't

said he felt that way, so neither could she. The line between what was fake and what was real had never quite
been cleared.

All she could do was trust her feelings.

She loved him. So she would help him.

'Julian…'

'Hmm?'

'I was thinking.'

'Should I be worried?' He smirked.

She rolled her eyes, and even though his were closed,
an amused chuckle rolled through his chest.

She didn't know how he would react to her next
words, and he must have picked up on her apprehension
because he said, 'Sunshine, you can tell me anything.'

'I didn't like something you said earlier.'

He opened his eyes to peer at her. 'What did I say?'

'That you blamed yourself.'

He took a deep breath but she pushed on.

'And I was thinking that you should visit your stepfather.'

His body went rigid. Any warmth lingering in his
stare dissipated. 'No.'

'Julian—'

He flung the covers away and got off the bed, pulling on his underwear with jerky movements. 'I'm not
seeing that man.'

'I think it could help you.'

She sat up, trying to reach for him, but he stepped out
of her path. She tried not to let the hurt show on her face.

'That man hurt my mother, Lily.'

His voice was low now. Dangerous. He was button-
ing his pants, snatching his crumpled shirt off the chair
in the corner of the light-filled room.

She didn't like it that he was getting dressed. It seemed too much as if he was erecting a barrier between them.

She vaulted out of bed, stepping between him and the door. 'Just please listen.'

'I'm not seeing that man and that's final.'

He stepped around her and went through the door, leaving her alone in the room.

She dressed as quickly as she could, in another one of his T-shirts, and set out in search of him. She had to try to convince him. Help him have closure so he could move on with his life. A life that until now had centred only around IRES.

He wasn't anywhere in the house. It was only when she went down to the lower level that she spied him on the terrace. Sitting on the edge of a pool lounger. Sunset rays glinting off his red hair. Elbows braced on his knees.

'Julian...' she said softly, sitting on the lounger next to his. An arm's length away. 'I just want you to be happy.'

He said nothing. Simply stared at the cement floor as if it contained some answer he was searching for.

'And you're not,' she went on. 'I see you—all of you—and I hate that you've been blaming yourself for something you shouldn't.'

She looked over at him, still he said nothing.

'I think talking to him now could give you some closure. Allow you to move on with your life.'

Lily sighed, looking across the Bay towards the bridge.

'I want so much more for you, Julian. More than just IRES. You deserve life, and you have so much of that in you, but you've got it all shackled. I want you to see that you're not like him. That you don't have to keep running from your past. Because it's only going to hold you back from what you could have. What you might want to have. I'm not presumptuous enough to believe that's me, but there's a whole world out there for you.'

She looked at him then, to find he was staring at her. Still silent, but listening at least.

'Please just think about it.'

She moved to stand up, wanting to leave him in peace, but his voice stopped her.

'I vowed never to go back there.' He was looking at the floor again. 'I'll think about it.'

Julian looked at the small bungalow. The blue paint that haunted his dreams was peeling away. The yard was overgrown with weeds. The windows were nearly opaque with crusted dirt.

His hands tightened around the steering wheel of the rental car.

Lily placed her hand on his shoulder. He didn't have a smile to give her. He had nothing right now. His shoulders were tense beneath his black suit.

This place brought back nightmares. He could still see himself entering the house for the first time. Could see his mother take her last breath. Julian would never have come back here at all. He had left Lupine Heights and everything in it behind. Yet Lily had said she didn't believe she was what he wanted, he'd wanted to scream. She was *all* he wanted and didn't deserve. So, for her, he would try. Try to put this place and this man behind him. And maybe then, for as long as she would let him, they could be happy together. Until she had to walk away.

Julian wasn't foolish enough to think it wouldn't end, because of course it would. He hadn't changed and neither had she. The stakes were still the same.

He tried to push all that away as he climbed out of the car. All he needed was for his stepfather to accept accountability for what he'd done. Nothing more.

He walked around the car, but Lily had already climbed out, was holding her hand out to him. He took it, keeping her a little behind him as they set off up the broken concrete path.

Climbing the stairs to the front door, he felt his stomach turn with disgust at the sight of the empty beer bottles all around the porch. Anger was growing within him, burning a trail through his veins.

He took a breath. He didn't lose control these days and he wouldn't give his stepfather the satisfaction of doing it now.

Raising a fist to the door, Julian knocked three times, then waited, shielding Lily just a little bit more with his body. He had asked her to stay behind, even though he'd wanted her with him. The idea that she should be around this vile man had made his stomach churn. But she'd refused, saying she wanted to be there for him just as he was for her. As much as he appreciated it, everything in him was now screaming to protect her.

'Well, well, well… Look who it is,' said the man with the sneering face who came to the door.

He was a head shorter than Julian, with cruel blue eyes that held no beauty at all, and he was portly, with a yellowish tinge to his skin and the whites of his eyes.

'Vincent.'

Julian had avoided saying that name as much as he could throughout his life.

'What do you want, boy?'

He felt Lily tense and couldn't blame her. No one else would dare speak to him this way.

'To talk.'

Vincent stepped aside, allowing them to enter, and a horrible sense of déjà vu overcame Julian as he stepped over the threshold into the dark house. It reeked of alcohol, stale cigarettes, and whatever it was that was rotting in the kitchen.

'You better sit, then.'

'We'll stand,' Julian said, looking down at a small brown stain on the carpet.

He could almost see a small, pretty woman curled around that spot.

'Suit yourself.' Vincent dropped into a couch, taking a swig from a half-empty bottle of whisky, watching them. He looked at Lily. 'What are you doing with *him*, sweetheart?'

'Don't you dare talk to her,' Julian growled.

He was burning. Burning from the inside out. Every shout and echoing through time in his head.

'Then what do you want?'

'For you to listen.'

Lily squeezed his fingers—a tether so that his fury didn't sweep him away.

'I left this place intending never to see it again, but the idea of you living your life in peace after what you did to my mother is not acceptable.'

Vincent scoffed, but Julian ignored him.

'I want you to admit what you did. What you did to my mother. Not just the beatings, but drinking away any money for her cancer treatment, what you did to me…all of it. I want you to take responsibility and then tell me why.'

Vincent huffed a remorseless laugh.

There was true evil in this world, Julian thought, and he had been raised by it. He never should have brought Lily here. Bright, sunny Lily, in her violet dress, with her loving heart and empathetic soul. She should never have had to set foot in this hell.

She let go of his hand and pressed herself into his side. Her arm moved around his waist and his around her shoulders.

Vincent's eyes narrowed.

'You want me to admit to what *I* did? What was that? Teach a runt some manners? Encourage my wife to behave as she should?'

Julian's hands curled into fists.

'Easy…' Lily whispered beside him.

'Maybe I was tough on you both, but look at you now.'

'Tough? You call what you did being *tough*? You killed her. You know that, don't you?'

Julian's voice was low and menacing. Anyone else would be cowering.

'What help were you?' Vincent threw back. 'All that intelligence and still your mother died. What use were you?'

Julian had no defence. Those were questions he had asked himself time and time again. Selfishly, he'd wanted time away from this house. Away from the bickering and abuse. And instead of using that time as he knew he should have, he'd just looked for an escape. He was just as responsible.

'You think you're so much better than me, boy? You forget I raised you. We're the same. Don't think I didn't see the enjoyment on your face that day.'

The day he'd fought back. As surprised as he'd been, he had enjoyed it. For a moment he'd made Vincent hurt and he'd revelled in it. Played it back in his mind several times in the days and weeks that had followed. A savage smile curling his lips every time he thought of it.

'I'm nothing like you, old man. I'm not the one who beat a woman and a child. I made something of my life.'

Vincent took another swig of whisky and the motion had Julian wanting to grab the bottle and shatter it across the wall.

'Maybe you did, but you're still a monster—no matter how fancy your suits or how rich you are. Remember that.'

'You're wrong.'

'Lily, don't.'

He frowned when she ignored him.

'He isn't a monster. He has never been one. But I can see all the lies you tried to fill his head with for so many years. I'm glad we came here today, so he could see exactly what he left behind. Exactly what he *isn't*.'

Julian couldn't help himself. He dropped a kiss to the top of her head. Just when he thought he couldn't love her any more, she did something like this and took his breath away.

He looked at his stepfather, once more prepared for this to be his last goodbye. 'How much time do you have left?' he asked.

'What?'

'The skin…the eyes. Yet you're still drinking. How much time do you have left?' Julian asked again.

'Maybe six months,' Vincent replied. 'Less.'

'You don't deserve this but you're getting it anyway. I'll make sure you get treatment at the local hospital. I'm not getting you a carer to abuse. You dug this hole for yourself, and you can die alone.'

Julian led Lily out of the house, saying nothing until they were both in the car. Leaning his head back, he gave himself a moment—just one—before starting the car and easing it into the road, not bothering to look back at the house disappearing behind him.

Vincent wasn't wrong. He was a monster. He'd been raised by one, after all.

CHAPTER FOURTEEN

VINCENT'S WORDS WERE still spinning around Julian's mind when they walked into the house. Nothing he'd said had been a surprise. They were all words he had said to himself.

Julian shrugged off his jacket, depositing it on the couch on the way to the massive window. It was dark over the water. Lights reflecting off the black surface.

'Julian?'

He spun around at the sound of Lily's voice. She had been so quietly supportive…hadn't said anything on the drive home. No offerings of hollow words. Simply a presence beside him.

'You know none of what he said is true, right?' she said softly, padding over to him.

He put his hands on her hips as soon as she was close enough to touch.

'None of it—I mean it.'

He closed his eyes for moment, but before he could say anything he was met with a very firm, 'Julian…'

He couldn't help but smile at that. Lily could see right through him and he had done nothing to deserve her.

'I want you to listen to me very carefully,' she said. 'Just because that man raised you, it does not mean you will turn out like him. *You* are kind and protective, Julian. The only monster is Vincent.'

How could he tell her that wasn't true? What kind of son didn't do everything in his power to help his mother? Looking back, he knew he'd had options to get them out. Or, when he'd become the main source of conflict, to remove himself from the equation. Maybe not at first, but afterwards he could have thought of something.

'Talk to me, please,' Lily begged, cupping his cheek.

'I know we're not the same, Sunshine. But that doesn't make me good,' he said softly.

He wasn't good. Not like her.

'Yes, you are. Please don't doubt that. I know today was hard...'

That was an understatement. To see his stepfather showing no remorse had infuriated Julian, and that tension still riddled his body, but he couldn't explode. He had no way to let it out.

'But you have to see how different you are. Will always be.'

'Lily, I'm nothing but darkness.'

'Julian, if it weren't for the darkness we'd never see the stars. Despite everything you've been through, your heart is pure. I feel safe with you, and I haven't felt that way in a long time.'

The words made a lump form in his throat, and all he could do was take her lips in his...swallow the gasp that made him burn for her. Sweetly, his lips roved over hers, sliding together and pulling apart. He felt her hand grip the shirt at his waist and he licked at the seam of her lips, which parted with a moan that had arousal arrowing through him.

He slid his hands down to her thighs, lifting her up, and then climbed the stairs to his bedroom, setting her back on her feet at the foot of his bed.

After everything that happened during the day, after Lily's words, Julian wanted only to ravish her. To mark her with his mouth. To have her scream his name, but he didn't deserve that. Neither did she. She should be worshipped.

Standing on the tips of her toes, Lily brought her lips up to his ears, sucking his earlobe into her mouth. He groaned.

'You once told me you're not gentle. Show me how not gentle you can be,' she whispered. 'Let go, Julian. Break free with me.'

Her teeth grazed the shell of his ear while she ran her nails down the front of his shirt, then down, down, down over the bulge in his pants, and his leash snapped free. He crashed his lips down on hers on a rushed breath. A hard, bruising kiss full of desperation and fervour. Then his tongue was in her mouth, and the clipped, uncontrolled noises she made just drove him wilder.

Teeth were tugging on her lip that she bit down on so often. Julian wanted to lay her out every time she did so. And then he was cutting a blazing trail with his own lips and tongue along her jaw, kissing that sensitive spot beneath her ear and feeling her shudder like it was his own. He moved down her neck to the hollow at the base of her throat. Licking, tasting the sweet skin there, as she threw her head back, offering herself up to him.

Julian pulled away. 'Do you have any attachment to this dress?' he asked, voice low, breaths uneven.

'No...'

'Good.'

The sound of tearing fabric rent the air, and before it had properly fluttered to the floor her bra had joined it. Arching her back in his arms, Julian closed his mouth over her nipple, sucking hard, making her mewl. But he didn't stop. Not when he was so enjoying the litany of gibberish that fell from her mouth.

And then he dropped to his knees, peeling her panties away and closing his mouth over her sex. Groaning at the obvious evidence of her arousal. Her honey taste.

His tongue was relentless. Her nails scraped against his scalp, delicate fingers tugging his hair, and it had him pulling her harder against him. She was swaying as if her muscles couldn't cope with the onslaught of pleasure, but he wanted more. Wanted to give more. So he hooked his arm tightly around her hips and slid a finger deep within her. The loud moan had satisfaction curling through him, pushing him to pleasure her until she exploded spectacularly.

Her body had gone limp. But he had her. Wouldn't let her fall.

He laid her on the bed, stomach down, and reached into his nightstand for a foil packet. Then he kissed her back, all the way up her spine. Brushing her hair aside, he kissed her nape. His hardness pressed against her entrance.

'Please, Julian...' Lily said breathily.

The words set his blood on fire.

He pushed into her, one arm moving under her to press her against his heat. His body curled protectively around hers as his hips set a merciless pace.

He cursed under his breath. 'Sunshine...' he moaned beside her ear.

God, he loved her! So much that he couldn't get close enough or have her fast enough. And then there was the way she said his name, over and over. Like a chant. Like a prayer. And it was all cracking him open. She was the only person he wanted to see him. To know him. All of him.

'I can't get enough of you, Sunshine…'

He threaded his fingers through hers, pressing her palms down onto the bed. The sheets pleated and curled in their joint fisted grip. This intensity of pleasure was a blow to his body and his mind with every thrust. But he needed to see her. To look into those obsidian eyes.

So he pulled away and turned her over…

Lily had wanted Julian to let go. She had seen from the moment they'd got in the car that he needed some sort of release. A means to explode. Because he was feeling too much and locking it all away.

And now he was unleashed. With her.

Beads of sweat coated his body. Every muscle was pulled taut. A predatory gleam in his eyes, but there was something more in that darkened gaze. She couldn't decide if she loved it more that he had opened himself to her, or that he was making her see stars.

He pushed all the way into her, banding both his arms around her body. They were pressed together, his head in the crook of her neck, and he was kissing her, whispering to her of her perfection, as his substantial length slid in and out of her at a rapid rate.

Lily didn't know any more if she was moaning or if her ragged breathing had just turned this loud. In Julian's embrace, surrounded by his heat and his scent and his voice, all she knew was a burning pleasure that had her heart thundering and her toes curling.

She wished she had known that she could feel like this. Feel taken and loved, safe and yet still dangling over a precipice. To feel so connected to someone and still lust after them.

'Mine.'

It was a guttural declaration that made Lily shiver.

'Yours,' she managed on a broken breath, and his arms seemed to hold her even tighter.

He was coming apart now—just as she was—in a firestorm. She couldn't get enough breath. They were going to set this whole house aflame. And those flames grew. From the depths of her, through her blood and her body, until she couldn't hold it at bay any longer. And she erupted just as she heard Julian's shout, felt his body tensing with hers. Rolling. Swaying. Holding on until they were both ash.

Limp.

Spent.

Bit by bit his grip loosened, as if he was coming back into his body and the animal was being caged away. He lifted his head, but only to press his forehead to hers, and she looked into glazed blue-green eyes and saw love and no small amount of caution.

He had let go, but she was still here. This bed, this home, was where she would always want to be, and tears slipped from her eyes at the realisation. She tried to dash them away, but he gently brushed them off her cheeks first.

She didn't know why she was crying. She was happy. Happier than she ever remembered being. Despite the tears, she smiled. Broadly. Warmly. As if the sunshine was inside her.

Her face lit up like the sun, squeezing the breath from his lungs. Lily was so beautiful. So pure. Utterly perfect.

What are you doing, Julian? he asked himself.

And he knew then that he had to end this right now. It couldn't go on a moment longer. He couldn't be the one to extinguish that light from her eyes. Because he would. He knew it. He was dark, violent, filled with rage, and she would never deserve that.

She deserved a good man. As much as he hated the idea of her with anyone but him, it was the truth. He didn't deserve her. And if he truly loved her he would let her go, so she could find a happy, free life.

But because he was weak, like his stepfather had always said he was, he let her pull him in for another kiss.

One more night. He'd give himself that. One more night.

So he lost himself in her lips and her scent and her sweet satin skin one last time.

CHAPTER FIFTEEN

Lily was fast asleep, curled against Julian, when he woke. Her scent was all around him. Pulling him under. Drowning him in everything he felt for her. This was a once-in-a-lifetime love. He knew it as he knew his own name. He loved her so much he couldn't breathe.

He had barely slept. When he had, he'd dreamed of her, and when he'd lain awake he'd held her close, as if she would disappear at any moment.

Mine.

That was what he had said the night before. The word played in his mind but he hadn't intended to say it out loud. And she had said she was his. He wanted that desperately— —but she couldn't be. Nothing had changed.

She turned towards him in her sleep and he pulled her against him, his fingers threading through her hair. Forehead pressed against hers. He loved her, and he knew she loved him too. It should have made him happy, but it was only breaking him apart.

Love wasn't enough. Not for him. It had done nothing to save the mother he'd loved, who had also loved his stepfather. The mother who had loved him so fiercely but who had never been able to choose him. It wasn't enough for her to leave Vincent. Not even after he had broken Julian's arm.

All that love but it didn't make him worthy. He hadn't been worthy enough for her to save, and he wasn't worthy enough for Lily.

Vincent had called him many things over the years. To Julian, they were all true. He had been weak when he was younger. He wasn't good enough, and he was most certainly selfish. Why else would he have taken Lily's affection, knowing there could never be anything between them? And now she'd returned that affection, but he was going to cut her loose and fade into memory.

He had to.

She hadn't chosen this relationship. She'd been thrust into it. By him. By his idea that they could use each other. But he had just used her desperation. He was going to make millions from their arrangement, and all she'd get was the life she was owed.

Opportunistic—that was what he was.

He had pulled her into his darkness. And there was only darkness in him. His soul hadn't seen light. Not until she'd walked in at least. Julian couldn't do this to her. He needed to protect her light. Couldn't let her be tainted by him. He just had to look at all that he had done. In life, in business, Julian *was* ruthless. He'd earned that reputation. Revelled in it until it became a problem. Until it had hurt IRES.

Now he didn't care about his company as much as he did Lily. He didn't know when that had happened. He just knew that his mother was gone but Lily could still be protected—even from him. He would walk away and make her do so too. She would find happiness without him. His heart was in pieces now, but he would do this. For her. Anything for her.

Julian held her against his body tightly. Trying to imprint her into his soul. She would always be there. There would be no one else.

Kissing her head, he silently said his goodbye to her. Scrunching up his eyes, clenching his jaw, Julian tossed aside the covers, careful not to wake her as he left the bed.

He watched her then. Hair fanning out over his pillow as she sought out his warmth in her slumber. Committing the way she looked to memory, Julian left the room.

He showered and changed into a dark suit in one of the guest rooms before going downstairs, where he would make the call he had hoped not to have to make. Since the Zenith dinner he had been called by several businessmen who had never shown any inclination to work with him before. As a result, several deals had been signed with IRES. But Julian knew the moment he broke up with Lily—the moment he broke her heart— the Arum deal would be lost. Devan's vote would be gone.

He didn't care. It would be a fitting punishment to lose it. Except his employees didn't deserve that. And, more importantly, Lily wouldn't be fooled into leaving.

Their agreement was that they would pretend until the deal was signed. Well, there was only one way he was getting that done now—and it wasn't through the support of the board.

He had his phone to his ear, waited three rings before it was answered by a hostile drawl.

'What do you want, Ford?'

'Harrison. I want the Arum energy deal and you're going to give it to me.'

Julian wished he didn't have to do this, but he did. He was already in bed with these people, and showing them just how ruthless he was would change nothing. All his contracts were iron clad, and once people worked with him they didn't look elsewhere.

'And why is that?' asked Lincoln.

'Two reasons,' he responded. 'One, you know how good I am. How good my technology is. You've already done the research and you know you would be a fool to discount IRES.'

He waited, but there was no denial.

'And two, I know you looked in to me the moment I spoke to Lily. I did the same the day you accosted her at Crème, and I am damn sure you don't want what I found out to become public knowledge.'

There was an amused huff on the line. 'Are you blackmailing me? You'll find nothing sticks to me, Ford.'

'I'm incentivising you to make the right choice, because you and I both know I can make your past misdeeds hurt. Do you really want to try me, Harrison?'

There was a long pause before Lincoln spoke again. 'You seem to think you're going to lose the other fifty percent of the vote. I wonder why that is.'

'Every good businessman has contingencies in place. I'll leave nothing to chance.'

'If you do lose the others' support, you realise my vote counts for exactly half.'

Of course Julian knew that. 'Yes, and I also know that you hold the tie breaker vote. So what will it be? Giving IRES the deal or facing your reckoning? I can

count your crimes if you'd like. Let's see…there's brib-
ery, assault of various degrees, that I'm sure you can
thank your father for burying. Then there's—'

'Enough. Fine. You'll have your deal, Ford, but this
won't be forgotten.'

'I'm sure it won't.'

Julian slipped the phone into his pocket and turned
around to find Lily descending the staircase, freshly
showered and ready to leave for work. Not just leaving for work, Julian reminded himself. This would be
the last time he saw her, and he had to fight the crum-
bling inside him.

'That was the news we've been waiting for. The
board has voted to go with IRES,' Julian said.

She walked over to him and kissed him lightly on
his cheek. It knocked the breath from him. He knew he
would never have that touch again, but he had to stand
firm and do at least one good thing in his life.

'That's wonderful news.' She smiled, but it faded
quickly, to be replaced by a frown. 'Julian, what's
wrong?'

'Nothing's wrong,' he said, taking a step back.

She tracked his movement.

'We've achieved what we set out to do,' he told her.

'I don't understand…'

'You've got what you wanted out of this arrangement
and now I have, too.'

'Arrange…? Are you breaking up with me?'

He would hate himself for the rest of his life for the
hurt he saw flash across her face. And it would only
get worse.

'Breaking up would imply there was something real
to begin with. It's time for you to leave.'

Julian's heart was tearing itself to shreds.

Don't leave. I need you.

But the thought would never be heard.

Her features had set in a determined look. The first time he'd seen it was when she'd walked over to him in a room full of people.

'A lamb to the slaughter,' he'd said that night.

'I know what you're doing,' she said. 'I won't leave you.'

'I want you to go.'

His ring was on her finger and yet he was pushing her away. This felt wrong. It was all wrong. But he had to do it. He would never make her happy—he wasn't capable of that. He'd let his mother die, failed her, but he could save Lily.

'Julian, don't do this. Please…'

Her eyes welled up, her voice breaking on that last word, but he wouldn't let himself comfort her. He would have to endure her hurt. Bear his punishment.

Julian shook his head and looked out through the window at the water stretching to the horizon.

'I'm a monster, Lily. Haven't you ever wondered why I never seem to have much competition? I put people out of business. You yourself brought up Helios. I do whatever I need to win.'

He turned back to her, removing any emotion from his voice. Making it as cold as he could manage. He was a good liar, after all.

'I've been doing that with you, too. So, please, just go.'

Her tears fell. 'You're not a monster…' She dashed the wetness away with the back of her hand. 'If this is about yesterday… You're not him. You're good and kind.'

'You've just seen what you want to, Lily.'

He couldn't call her 'Sunshine'. Not now. It would undo him.

'Vincent was right. I did enjoy beating the shit out of him. And he wasn't the only one. That's who I am. I told you at the start I'm not the hero of this story. And I'm telling you for the last time—leave. I don't want you.'

He saw her throat bob as she lifted her chin. She wouldn't beg, and he was so proud of her. She was strong. She would be fine. And since Lincoln had moved on, he was no longer a threat either.

'Fine.'

She prised the ring off her finger and he couldn't bear it.

'Take it back,' she said.

'No. Keep it.'

He wanted to say that it was part of their plan, but really it was just his selfish need to have her never forget him.

She curled her fingers around it, regarding him with those remarkable eyes. 'Thank you for what you've done for me, Julian. Good luck with IRES. I'll send for my things.'

Without so much as a goodbye, she turned around. And he watched the woman he loved walk out of his house.

The walls were closing in. His clothes felt too tight. Too constricting. He couldn't breathe. Something was trying to break free of him.

He watched the door. And he watched, and he watched—until he snapped, flipping the glass table over and sending it crashing to the floor, shattering in a snowfall of razor-sharp ice.

She was gone.

And he was alone in his house. Just as he had always preferred.

CHAPTER SIXTEEN

LILY COUNTED THE number of steps to the door, then to her car. She kept counting. Anything…*anything* to keep her from falling apart. To stop her from focussing on the man she was leaving behind. The man who didn't want her. Who had never said this was real.

Except she had felt it. She had felt his love with every touch the night before. But if he couldn't take that step towards her, she wouldn't force him. If he wanted to be left alone, then he would be.

It was that thought of never seeing him again that had the first tear falling.

Fracturing. Her heart, her soul…it was all fracturing. A fissure was opening up right through her, and into it fell all the memories they'd made. She couldn't think of any of them.

Starting up her car, Lily took a deep breath and drove away from the house. Not to Crème, but to her brother. Why? She had no idea. He hadn't been a supportive brother lately. But she had just lost her home—not the spectacular house perched on a cliff, but the man who lived in it—and maybe she craved something familiar. Something that might once have been comforting.

She drove along the street she had grown up on and

turned into the drive of what was now her brother's home. She took a moment, trying to breathe around the suffocating knot in her chest, but every breath hurt. As if she was choking on it.

Still, she tried not to let the tears fall. Because if she started, she likely wouldn't stop.

Fishing the key she had not returned out of her bag, Lily reached for the lock—only to have the door swing open. And there, ready to start his day, stood Devan.

'Lily?' Surprise turned to concern, and then to anger.

'Dev…' she managed hoarsely, through the burning in her throat, and let out a muffled sob when he pulled her into a crushing hug.

'What happened?' he asked.

She swallowed, opening and closing her mouth several times, but no words came out. So much had happened. A lifetime fitted into such a short period. And all those memories she'd thought had fallen into that fissure now crashed upon her.

Devan led her to the kitchen, let her perch on one of the tall chairs around the large marble island where they used to spend their time. They hadn't shared the same space in an age.

She watched her brother shed his jacket and take the seat next to her.

She toyed with the ring on her finger. Big and beautiful and sparkling. She pulled it off, turning it around and around between her fingers.

'He called it off.'

She didn't look at her brother. Didn't want to see the smug satisfaction on his face. It had probably been a mistake, her coming here.

'He couldn't do it,' she said in a small voice.

He couldn't accept that he was good. Had pushed her away because of it.

'I knew he would hurt you,' Devan said lowly. 'He never deserved you. Don't worry, Lily, I can make him pay.'

'No!' she rushed out. He had been hurt enough. 'Don't ruin the deal for him, please.'

'How can you ask me that?'

'Because a lot has happened, Dev. Julian…' Something caved within her just at saying his name. 'He's a good man. He just has his own battles to fight.'

Still she didn't give up that ring. She was supposed to keep wearing it until the time was right to take it off. The time would never be right because all she wanted was to tie herself to him. She accepted him. All of him.

Over and over he'd said he was the villain, but he wasn't. No matter what he did, she loved every part of him. Yet she couldn't keep his ring on her finger because it hurt too much to see it there.

'You love him…' Devan said, sounding almost as if he still didn't truly believe it.

'I do.'

'I have to admit, Lil…part of me hoped that this was all some sort of elaborate game.'

Guilt slammed through her. Maybe that was how it had started, but she thought back to their first date and realised it hadn't ever been. Not really. She and Julian had been special from the start and now it was over. It was always meant to end, and she should have done a better job of barricading her heart.

'I don't want to talk about him.' She sniffed. She couldn't bear it. She missed him already—as if a piece of her soul had been ripped away.

'He was my home, Dev. No one cared for me like he did.'

Devan flinched, then shifted closer. 'I haven't been a very good brother to you, have I?'

'No, you haven't,' she said softly, and saw him wince.

'I hate seeing you hurt, Lily. And I'm sorry that I was also a cause of it.'

Lily said nothing, focussing instead on the way the sunlight danced on the diamond.

'I have no excuse,' he went on. 'I guess I wanted to do right by Dad. I had something to prove. But I should have been there for you. I should have helped you with Lincoln. That should never have been placed on your shoulders. I'm sorry I tried to force you.'

Lily finally looked at her brother, seeing genuine remorse on his face. 'What are you going to do about him?' she asked.

'Don't worry about it. I'll find a way.'

He snaked an arm around her and she rested her head on his shoulder.

'I've missed you, Dev.'

'I've missed you too, Lily.'

Julian sat behind his desk in his office, high above San Francisco, just as he had done for the last three weeks. The rest of the floor was dark. Everyone had left hours ago. Not one of them, not even his PA, had said goodbye. They had all been giving him a wider berth than usual.

The sky behind him was pitch-black. Twinkling lights spread out as far as the eye could see. He had no mind for it. No mind for the beauty. It didn't matter. All that mattered was his work.

In the weeks since Lily had left, Julian had focussed only on IRES and he had been productive. Of course he had, when he'd had to keep busy every waking hour. It was all he could do to stop himself thinking about Lily. To spend as little time as he could in that bed where they had come together every night. In his home that now felt too big. Too empty.

His life was empty without her, but he couldn't let himself dwell on the ache in his chest that hadn't let up since he'd made her leave. He had always known he would have to let her go, and still he'd let himself love her. Still, he'd carried that love in every breath.

His phone rang, pulling him out of the thoughts he had fallen into. Thoughts of Lily. Glancing at the screen, he let it go to voicemail. If it wasn't about work, he didn't need to hear it.

It didn't help that while people suspected they were no longer together, Lily hadn't said anything to anyone. So everyone asked how was she? Where was she? What was going on? And every time he barked that it was none of their business.

He scrubbed a hand down his face, barely able to keep his eyes open any longer. Grabbing his laptop, he left his office, went down to his car and drove home in silence, mentally planning out his next day.

IRES had been awarded the Arum deal. It was a massive undertaking, which thankfully kept him busy. And, as reluctant a partnership as it was, Lincoln was clearly impressed with what Julian had brought to the table.

But it felt like a hollow victory.

He had wanted to earn his way in. Show the elite just what his company could do and make them choose him. After all, if these contracts were handed out on merit, there would never be any doubt that IRES would be their first choice every time. Except they weren't. And Julian had had to resort to ruthless means once again. It had been the only way to ensure his goal and thereby set Lily free.

His home loomed dark and unwelcoming as he parked his car in the underground garage. He wondered, as he walked into the house and went straight to the fridge, what Lily would have said if she'd known what he'd done to get the contract.

'Don't do anything that could hurt you later.'

Her voice in his head made him flinch. He had already done that, even though it had been for the best. One day she would find someone who loved her—not as much as he did…no one could love her like him. Someone who would make her happy.

Julian slammed the door shut. His appetite had disappeared in an instant.

He dragged himself up the stairs, feeling more like a shadow than ever before, and let out a heavy breath before entering his room. He could have avoided it—just like he'd avoided going anywhere near Crème. He did have other rooms that would have suited him.

But he was stuck here. Wanting the memories of her and the freedom this room had been meant to grant him. But all it had become was a prison he'd sentenced himself to.

CHAPTER SEVENTEEN

A WEEK LATER, Julian was home before dark for the first time since Lily had left. He'd barely had a moment to place his belongings down when the doorbell chimed. He knew who it was before he opened the door, and when he did so his mentor's concerned expression greeted him.

'Henry.'

'It's been weeks, Julian.'

It had been. He'd sent Henry's calls to voicemail more often than not, and when he had spoken to him it had usually been to postpone whatever plans Henry had included him in.

After weeks of being cancelled on, it seemed he'd had enough.

Julian stood aside, holding the door open to allow Henry to enter. 'I've been busy.'

Henry didn't seem convinced.

Julian led him to the plush couches out on the pool terrace, where the two men sat opposite each other.

'You've been busy since you were a teenager, Julian. This is about Lily, isn't it?'

Julian looked away. Past the thick trees that offered him complete privacy and over the water.

'Tell me the truth this time,' Henry said, and there was a softness in his voice that made Julian grit his teeth.

Of course Henry had seen through the ruse, even though he had never said anything. Likely he'd been waiting for Julian to sort out his own mess.

He swallowed, thinking of the night he'd first seen Lily, and then he said, 'It was just meant to be a convenient arrangement. A mutually beneficial one.'

'It was more than that,' Henry said, as if it was an undeniable truth.

'Yes.'

Julian ached. He missed Lily so much it was a physical pain. He walked to the edge of the pool, staring at nothing in particular, and slid his hands into his pockets. Lily was gone. It would make no difference if he told Henry about it now. So he did. Leaving his feelings well and truly out of it.

'Julian,' Henry said when he'd finished, but he refused to turn around. 'I know you love her. Look at what you did. You wanted into Zenith, wanted a deal with the man whose—for all intents and purposes—fiancée you took from right under his nose and threatened him, then blackmailed him. You made an enemy of the client you wanted to attract and I can tell part of you still wishes to destroy him. You took Lily from her home that she shared with her brother knowing what was at stake, telling yourself she'd help you get closer to Devan, accepted by him and his clique. It was never about any of that. Just admit that you wanted her from the moment you saw her. No matter what you've been over the years, son, you were always honest. So be honest now.'

Still Julian said nothing, because Henry was right.

'I knew she was special when I saw you two together,' said Henry. 'You realise that was the first time I ever saw you smile? I've known you all this time and finally I got to see you happy because of her. Look at you, Julian…you're a ghost of your former self.'

'I do love her,' Julian said finally, in a calm voice. 'That's why she had to go. I don't deserve her.'

'Julian…'

'Don't tell me it's not true. You're right. I'm not happy. But I couldn't take her happiness away for my own.'

'Did she tell you she was unhappy?' Henry challenged.

'She didn't need to. I had a reminder of who I really am, and I couldn't do that to her. I failed my mother, Henry. What if I do the same to her?'

The visit with Vincent was still fresh in his mind. Though he never intended to see the man again, his medical bills had been steadily flowing to him. They kept the wound open. Wouldn't let that last interaction fade into the background.

'What sort of reminder?'

'I saw Vincent.' Julian glanced over his shoulder to see the frown on Henry's face replaced by something fiercer. Anger.

'You know better than to listen to that…' Henry floundered, unable to find a word to adequately describe Julian's stepfather.

'He was right.' Julian looked away again. 'What use was this intellect when I didn't use it to help my mother? I could have. Instead of being selfish, and trying to find ways to stay away, *I* could have done something. But I didn't. I couldn't risk being that selfish again, Henry.'

'Julian…' Henry's tone was firm now. In a way it had never been with him before.

'He was right,' Julian repeated. 'Vincent did raise me. I'm every bit the monster he is. How could I not be? He is what I know. What if one day I lose control and turn into him? That's a possibility. We both know I have that violence in me.'

Julian's greatest fear. The possibility of becoming his stepfather scared him senseless. It was the reason he had to keep himself in check all the time. He had so much anger and resentment in him—where would a slip lead him? He'd still been a teenager when he'd put someone in hospital.

'You forget that I know you,' said Henry. 'You didn't leave it at that. What did you do?'

Julian dropped his head. 'Nothing. I did nothing.'

He had gone in wanting him to acknowledge what he had done to Julian and his mother, but he hadn't pushed for it.

'He's dying,' Julian said after a while. 'His liver is failing. I told him I'd pay his medical expenses and left.'

'Julian, sit,' Henry instructed.

He looked over his shoulder at his mentor with a cocked brow. Neither backed down until Julian let out a long breath and dropped into the couch opposite him.

Henry sat forward. His brown eyes were hard. It was a look Julian had seen him use in business.

'Now, you're going to listen to me. None of what Vincent accused you of is true. Yes, you may have been raised by him in part, but you were always your own person. You tried to protect your mother, but protection is an adult's job, and you were a child. I know you like to take responsibility, but you can't do that for everyone's actions. *You are not to blame*.'

Julian rubbed his eyes with his forefinger and thumb but didn't interrupt.

'You are a good man, Julian. Better than you realise. You helped that scum and left. Do you know what strength that takes? And what about Lily? You helped her because you wanted to. I'm willing to bet you would have even without the Arum deal hanging over you.'

He would have. Of that Julian had no doubt.

'You have accomplished so much, but until now, you have only been surviving. And you're barely doing that right now. You need to live, Julian. Let yourself be happy. Did you not let go just a little with Lily?'

'I did,' he admitted, thinking back to how she had unleashed him and hadn't turned away.

'Your happiness isn't a crime. It's okay to be ruthless in business—you need to be—but not in your life. Don't cut things out that bring you joy because of a fear you shouldn't have to bear.'

'I pushed her away, Henry. I doubt she would want to see me.'

He could still picture her hurt when he'd told her to leave. For that alone, he was the villain.

'You know Crème has the best *cannelé*?' Henry smiled.

'You saw her?' Julian breathed.

'I did. Don't worry. I said nothing to her. I went only to check in.'

'How is she?'

'Miserable. She misses you too.'

His heart fluttered back to life. She missed him. Despite what he had done. Could he allow himself to see her? See if she still loved him. But what then?

'You know, there aren't many regrets I have in life,' said Henry. 'Hardly any, in fact. However, I do regret never settling down. Starting a family. I wish that I had. I got lucky, though. I found a son on a campus.'

Julian smiled at that. It was small and quick, but it felt like waking up from a haze. Henry had been there for him from the moment they'd met. Taken him in. Taught him. And, Julian realised, protected him. Helped him succeed. He had done everything a father would have done for his son.

'Vincent is not your father,' Lily had said, and Julian had been so hung up on all the ways he might have been that he hadn't seen what was right in front of him. Vincent had never been his father. Never his role model. He fought everything the man was. But Henry…

In every way that mattered, Henry was his father. Julian listened to him, emulated him when he could, had moved to San Francisco to be closer to him. Why had it taken him so long to see it? He couldn't have loved the man more even if he was blood.

'Not many people get that lucky,' Henry went on. 'You might not because you have something special in front of you right now. Are you going to let the woman you love slip through your fingers?'

He didn't want to. No part of him wanted to say goodbye to Lily but it was so hard to think of himself as someone worthy of her. What if he hurt her? He couldn't survive that. What if one day he grew angry and lost his temper with her just like Vincent had done? That would be unforgivable. Except he really wasn't like Vincent, was he? His darkness grew out of hatred and pain, but he always tried to be better than his stepfather. Tried to be more like Henry. The man who was looking at him with love and pride. Even when he had made a mistake Henry never turned his back on him.

If a man like Henry was willing to believe in Julian, why wasn't he willing to believe in himself? With Lily, he was everything he'd ever wanted to be. She brought out the best in him and he loved her. So much that he was willing to let her go and find love with someone else. He'd suffer for it, but he'd be at peace knowing she was happy.

Except she wasn't, from what Henry had said, and if being together could make them both happy why should he keep punishing himself? Punishing them both?

Their love wouldn't be like his mother's. It wouldn't be a trap filled with torment. His and Lily's love was something bright and pure.

'No, I'm not.'

He looked at his watch. If he rushed, he could make it to Crème before Lily closed up.

'You can lock up on your way out.'

Henry sat back, his expression a mixture of smugness and pride.

Julian paused on his way inside the house and threw over his shoulder, 'I met my father that day too, Henry.'

Crème was still open when Julian came to a screaming stop in a parking bay close to the entrance. Relief, fear and excitement all coursed through him in equal measure. It had been weeks since he had last seen Lily, and as he got out of his car and quietly walked into the store a strange sense of peace overcame him. The feeling of coming back home after a long time away.

He watched her smiling at customers, but the moment they left that smile vanished. He had done that, and he would beg her forgiveness for it.

She didn't look up. Not once. Paying attention instead to the display she was refilling, her back turned to him. For a moment he was frozen. Stuck on everything he should say. On whether she would let him say the words. If she would let him hold her.

'How much are the cinnamon rolls?' he asked, in his low voice over her shoulder.

Lily whipped around. Surprise, happiness, anger, sadness—all passed over her face in quick succession. A rainbow of emotion that ended with nothing…just a blank look when she saw him standing before her in jeans and a sweater.

'Julian.' Her voice was careful. 'What are you doing here?'

His heart beat frantically. He wanted her back, but it had to be her choice. He would lay himself bare to her and then she could decide if he was worthy. Whatever her decision, he would accept it. But he had to try.

'I needed to see you. Talk to you.'

She shook her head. Swallowed once. Then twice. 'It's been weeks, Julian. I think the time to talk is gone.'

She pushed past him to the door, which she locked, flipping the sign to closed. She tried to walk past him again, but he grabbed her wrist, making her stop.

'Please listen to me and after that I'll go. Will you allow that?'

A light sweat broke out at the back of his neck.

'You didn't want me. You told me to leave,' she said, pulling out of his grasp.

He tried to hide his wince. It hurt that she'd moved

away from him, but if he was honest he deserved it. 'I lied. I had to. I told you that you had no idea how good a liar I was.'

'Was?'

He nodded. 'I'm done with lying to myself…to you… to the world. I wanted you from the moment I laid eyes on you, Lily.'

She regarded him coolly. Carefully concealing her feelings from him. And now he understood how she'd felt when she had wanted him to let go. To give up his control and just feel. Because he wanted so badly for her to yell at him, or pound her fists on his chest. Anything but this stillness.

'Fine. Say what you came here to say and then you can leave.'

'Thank you.'

He wanted to reach for her, but didn't think she would appreciate that after the way he had behaved, so he took a deep breath instead.

'There was once a boy who knew only darkness and grief and pain. He was told he was brilliant, but all he felt was hopelessness. Each day was the same. Each day he had to fight that same darkness until he was consumed by it. He didn't know if he was still fighting it or if it was inside him any more, so he grew up trying his best. But with each passing day hate and pain were the only things that grew. Eventually whatever light was left in him was extinguished and that left only darkness. And so he believed that was what he was…that he didn't deserve the light.'

Lily was looking at him with a mix of concern and sympathy—and no small amount of anger. Not at him, though. He could tell. It was the same way she'd looked at him the night he'd told her about his past.

'I wanted to send you away because I had to save you from my darkness,' he told her. 'Do you know why I call you Sunshine?'

Lily shook her head.

'Because that's exactly what you are. What you've always been. My sunshine. You bring light to my very dark life, Lily. You make me see a path…a life that I couldn't see in that black void I lived in.'

'You're not filled with darkness, Julian,' she said brokenly.

He ran his thumb down her cheek, giving her a sad smile. 'Yes, I am. I've lost everything good in my life, so I was convinced that it was just a matter of time before I lost you too. The way I grew up…it was chaos. So I controlled everything. But you, Sunshine, bring order to my life—and yet at the same time the most beautiful chaos.'

Lily took a step towards him, closing the distance between them and he could have dropped to his knees.

'I just wanted to give you a chance to live a happy life on your terms,' he said. 'To save you from me. So that day, when I told you I would make sure Lincoln paid for hurting you, I started looking into him and I dug up a lot of dirt.'

Lily's eyes turned hard. But he was prepared for that.

'I told you not to do anything you'd regret,' she said.

'I know you did. So I sat on that information until the morning when I knew you had to go. I called Lincoln and told him I would use what I'd found if IRES didn't get the Arum deal.'

'You didn't need to do that,' she said in a hard tone.

'I didn't think I would have a chance with them after I sent you away. I didn't care about the deal anymore, but I knew you wouldn't leave me in the lurch. But we had an agreement, so the only way I could get you to leave was to get that contract. I did what I thought I had to.'

'Why didn't you just talk to me?' she asked.

'Because I wanted the best for you and I didn't think it was me.'

She scrunched her fingers in her ponytail and he watched her trying to sort through everything he'd told her.

'You shouldn't have done that,' she said.

'I know.'

'I wish you had talked to me about this, Julian. After we saw Vincent I blamed myself for pushing you too hard. But all I wanted was for you to get closure.'

'I needed that push, because you were right. But what he said was everything I had already said to myself. All the reasons I hated myself.'

'I wish you could see yourself clearly,' she said, her eyes welling up. 'I wish you could stop punishing yourself and live.'

'I want to—but I can't do this alone. Living instead of surviving. I thought I could, but I need you. You're my light when everything in me is just the darkest night. You give me hope that I can be a better man. Maybe even a good man. I love you, but I don't know how to do this.'

'You love me?'

Her tears finally fell free, cutting him to the quick. Julian took her face in his hands. He should have told her every moment of every day that he loved her.

'Yes! With everything I am. I want to protect you, and care for you, and take a ridiculous number of trips to France with you, and sit at that table—' he pointed to the spot where they had shared a meal on their second date '—eating dessert with you.'

'Julian…' Lily let out a sob. She loved him too. Had never stopped—not once in these long weeks.

'But I want…' Julian trailed off.

She had never seen him stumble or struggle for words, but she understood then. No one had chosen Julian. Not his mother, who tried to protect him but not leave for him, not his stepfather, who had so terribly hurt him, and definitely not all the business people who'd excluded him for no reason.

'You want me to choose you,' she said.

Julian didn't answer. She could see that he couldn't. Those blue-green eyes were flat. There was no mischief or humour or sadness. Just nothing reflected back at her. It broke her heart that he was too wary to ask for what he wanted but he never had. It was time he finally understood the depth of her feelings for him.

'Julian, I chose you from the start.' When he was still a beautiful stranger. She had left Lincoln's side and went to him that first night. His eyes twinkled at the memory. 'I'll always choose you. But I knew it was all just meant to be fake.'

That was the reason why she had never said she loved him.

'It was never fake for me,' he said earnestly. 'That first night, Lily, I saw you walk in with Devan and I felt kissed by the sun. I couldn't stop looking at you. Watching to see where you would go and what you would do.

I thought I loved you when I kissed you in your office. Knew I loved you when I took you to bed, and again that next morning. I let myself believe it when we went to France, and I hoped...*hoped* you could see it in what you did to me.'

Lily's last defences against Julian crumbled. She wanted him to be hers for the rest of her life.

She threw her arms around his neck, hugging him fiercely, felt his arms tighten around her the instant she did. 'I love you.'

Julian's head tucked into her neck. When he spoke his voice was muffled against her skin.

'You're my sunrise. My first spring blossom. My hope and my happiness. You give my world colour and meaning. You're everything I don't deserve but desperately want. You make me believe—and I love you so damn much!'

Lily felt as if a fog had lifted. As if the sun had finally come out and warmed her soul. Maybe she was light but Julian wasn't darkness, he was the darkest night sky in a remote location. Maybe he was hard to reach, but once she did, his beauty was breathtaking.

'You're the best person I know, Julian, and I love you, too.'

He pulled away from her embrace, only to kiss her hungrily. Impatient and uncontrolled. Showing her just how naked he could be with her, how much he loved her, and she felt it. It was in the press of his lips and the touch of his tongue. In his hands fisted against her back and his tightly shut eyes.

She would stop the clocks so they could spend this moment tangled in each other for eternity, but he slowed the slide of his lips and broke the connection. He pressed his forehead against hers, his breath uneven.

'Do you still have my ring?' he asked hoarsely.

'I do. Do you want it back?'

'No. When you're ready to be my fiancée again—whether it's a day from now, or a week or a month or a year, I want you to leave it in the middle of our bed and I'll know you're ready. You'll have to say nothing else.'

He was giving her the choice. Letting her make the decision about her future. Their future. And she knew if there was ever a way for him to prove how much he loved her, respected her, it was this.

'What if I'm ready now?' Lily asked with a broad smile.

Julian chuckled, his breath brushing against her lips. 'Then we'll go home right now and you can show me that you want me.'

'Home? I've bought my own apartment, Julian.'

'*You're* my home, Sunshine. Whether it's my house—*our* house—or your new apartment, it's home.'

Those words made butterflies take flight in her stomach. Made her so happy she had to make sure she wasn't glowing.

Lily stood on tiptoe to whisper in Julian's ear. 'Race you there.'

EPILOGUE

One year later

THE SUN STREAMED into the pavilion at Strawberry Hill, cutting dark shapes into the floor. Stow Lake glittered beyond, but Lily could barely remember where she was. Nor could she pay attention to the small, intimate gathering of friends and family seated a few feet away from her.

She looked at her hands, held in Julian's grasp, trying not to let her vision blur with tears. Slowly, she raked her gaze up to meet his and, just like every time she did, her breath caught. In his tux, with his earring twinkling and the sun gilding him in golden light, he was magnificent. And he was hers. In every way. From this moment on.

Lily had thought she was happy before, but it was nothing compared to how she felt now.

The officiant said something she could not parse because she was still spellbound by Julian. And in a few minutes he would be her husband.

He had once told her he couldn't make her happy, but he'd been so wrong. Every day was happier than the last, and they were only just starting their fairy-tale.

It had only been a year, but so much had happened in that time. Lily had opened a dessert bar, to rave reviews, she and Devan had completely repaired their relationship, and her mother had moved back to San Francisco. Things weren't perfect there, but they were working on it. She'd even rekindled the friendships that she'd been certain she had lost. Her friends had welcomed her back with more than a few tears. And those same friends now sat amongst the small crowd sharing this day with them.

And Julian... He had worked every single day to show her how much he loved her. He had finally stopped blaming himself for his mother's death and accepted that he was nothing like his stepfather. While he was still supremely disciplined, he had started to relax. Let go a little. There was still a long way to go, but she planned to hold his hand throughout it all.

'Julian and Lily have prepared their own vows,' the officiant said now, and turned to Julian.

'Lily, I promise to always protect you. To support you in all that you do. To listen to you.'

He smiled broadly, dimples appearing in his cheeks, and her heart stuttered.

'To be your best friend and closest ally, just as you are mine, and I promise to give myself to you wholly in every way.'

He already had. Julian kept nothing from her. Let her see his bad days and nightmares and she loved him all the more for it. She thought back to the surprise that awaited him at the house. The pregnancy test she had taken the night before and couldn't wait to tell him about.

'Julian...' Her voice was thick with tears. 'I promise

to always choose you. To support you in all that you do. To listen to you. To be your best friend and closest ally, just as you are mine, and I promise to give myself to you wholly in every way.'

Julian couldn't stop looking at Lily. At her curled hair with the pretty flowers braided through it, at the beaded, toga-like dress, white against her golden skin, with the sun shining through the long drapes of fabric. At her night-sky eyes, glistening with tears. She was a goddess and she was his. Though not his alone.

Julian knew about the pregnancy test, but he would wait for her to tell him the way she wanted to. They were going to have a baby which would be perfect in every way, because it would be a part of her. He couldn't wait for its arrival—which, judging by how flat Lily's stomach was, would be a long way away.

'I love you, Sunshine…always,' he said, sealing his promise by sliding on to her finger a diamond wedding band that perfectly matched the engagement ring that had started them on this journey.

'I love you, Julian…unconditionally and for ever.'

A tear slipped down her cheek and he brushed it away with his thumb. He would never tire of hearing those words. He offered her his hand, and she slipped a simple titanium band on his finger. The weight was satisfying. Calming. Like a piece of him clicking into place.

'Titanium,' she had said. 'Because it doesn't break easily. It's strong…just as you are.'

He'd had no words for her then, and he wondered if he would wake up every day just as pleasantly surprised that he got to spend his life with Lily—his wife.

He took her face in his hands as her fingers curled around the lapels of his jacket and he kissed her. Softly, sweetly, gently. With all the love he held in his heart.

For the rest of their days their life would be perfect, he knew. Because right now he vowed to make sure of it.

* * * * *

If you fell in love with the magic of
Their Diamond Ring Ruse
then you'll be head over heels for these other
Bella Mason stories!

Awakened by the Wild Billionaire
Secretly Pregnant by the Tycoon

Available now!

#4137 NINE MONTHS TO SAVE THEIR MARRIAGE
by Annie West

After his business-deal wife leaves, Jack is intent on getting their on-paper union back on track. He just never imagined their reunion would be *scorching*. Or that their red-hot Caribbean nights would leave Bess *pregnant*! Is this their chance to finally find happiness?

#4138 PREGNANT WITH HER ROYAL BOSS'S BABY
Three Ruthless Kings
by Jackie Ashenden

King Augustine may rule a kingdom, but loyal assistant Freddie runs his calendar. There's no task she can't handle. Except perhaps having to tell her boss she's going to need some time off...because in six months she'll be having *his* heir!

#4139 THE SPANIARD'S LAST-MINUTE WIFE
Innocent Stolen Brides
by Caitlin Crews

Sneaking into ruthless Spaniard Lionel's wedding ceremony, Geraldine arrives just in time to see him being jilted. But Lionel is still in need of a convenient wife...and innocent Geraldine suddenly finds *herself* being led to the altar!

#4140 A VIRGIN FOR THE DESERT KING
The Royal Desert Legacy
by Maisey Yates

After years spent as a political prisoner, Sheikh Riyaz has been released. Now it's Brianna's job to prepare him for his long-arranged royal wedding. But the forbidden attraction flaming between them tempts her to cast duty—and her *innocence*!—to the desert winds...

#4141 REDEEMED BY MY FORBIDDEN HOUSEKEEPER

by Heidi Rice

Recovering from a near-deadly accident, playboy Renzo retreated to his Côte d'Azur estate. Nothing breaks through his solitude. Until the arrival of his new yet strangely familiar housekeeper, Jessie, stirs dormant desires...

#4142 HIS JET-SET NIGHTS WITH THE INNOCENT

by Pippa Roscoe

When archaeologist Evelyn needs his help saving her professional reputation, Mateo reluctantly agrees. Only the billionaire hadn't bargained on a quest around the world... From Spain to Shanghai, each city holds a different adventure. Yet one thing is constant: their intoxicating attraction!

#4143 HOW THE ITALIAN CLAIMED HER

by Jennifer Hayward

To save his failing fashion house, CEO Cristiano needs the face of the brand, Jensen, to clean up her headline-hitting reputation. But while she's lying low at his Lake Como estate, he's caught between his company...and his desire for the scandalous supermodel!

#4144 AN HEIR FOR THE VENGEFUL BILLIONAIRE

by Rosie Maxwell

Memories of his passion-fueled night with Carrie consume tycoon Damon. Until he discovers the ugly past that connects them and pledges to erase every memory of her. Then she storms into his office...and announces she's carrying his child!

Get 3 FREE REWARDS!

We'll send you 2 FREE Books <u>plus</u> a FREE Mystery Gift.

PRESENTS

His Innocent for
One Spanish Night

CAROL MARINELLI

PRESENTS

Bound by the
Italian's "I Do"

MICHELLE SMART

FREE
Value Over
$20

Both the **Harlequin® Desire** and **Harlequin Presents®** series feature compelling novels filled with passion, sensuality and intriguing scandals.

YES! Please send me 2 FREE novels from the Harlequin Desire or Harlequin Presents series and my FREE gift (gift is worth about $10 retail). After receiving them, if I don't wish to receive any more books, I can return the shipping statement marked "cancel." If I don't cancel, I will receive 6 brand-new Harlequin Presents Larger-Print books every month and be billed just $6.30 each in the U.S. or $6.49 each in Canada, a savings of at least 10% off the cover price, or 3 Harlequin Desire books (2-in-1 story editions) every month and be billed just $7.83 each in the U.S. or $8.43 each in Canada, a savings of at least 12% off the cover price. It's quite a bargain! Shipping and handling is just 50¢ per book in the U.S. and $1.25 per book in Canada.* I understand that accepting the 2 free books and gift places me under no obligation to buy anything. I can always return a shipment and cancel at any time by calling the number below. The free books and gift are mine to keep no matter what I decide.

Choose one: ☐ **Harlequin Desire**
(225/320 BPA GRNA)

☐ **Harlequin Presents Larger-Print**
(176/376 BPA GRNA)

☐ **Or Try Both!**
(225/326 & 176/376 BPA GRQP)

Name (please print)

Address   Apt. #

City   State/Province   Zip/Postal Code

Email: Please check this box ☐ if you would like to receive newsletters and promotional emails from Harlequin Enterprises ULC and its affiliates. You can unsubscribe anytime.

Mail to the Harlequin Reader Service:
IN U.S.A.: P.O. Box 1341, Buffalo, NY 14240-8531
IN CANADA: P.O. Box 603, Fort Erie, Ontario L2A 5X3

Want to try 2 free books from another series? Call 1-800-873-8635 or visit www.ReaderService.com.

*Terms and prices subject to change without notice. Prices do not include sales taxes, which will be charged (if applicable) based on your state or country of residence. Canadian residents will be charged applicable taxes. Offer not valid in Quebec. This offer is limited to one order per household. Books received may not be as shown. Not valid for current subscribers to the Harlequin Presents or Harlequin Desire series. All orders subject to approval. Credit or debit balances in a customer's account(s) may be offset by any other outstanding balance owed by or to the customer. Please allow 4 to 6 weeks for delivery. Offer available while quantities last.

Your Privacy—Your information is being collected by Harlequin Enterprises ULC, operating as Harlequin Reader Service. For a complete summary of the information we collect, how we use this information and to whom it is disclosed, please visit our privacy notice located at corporate.harlequin.com/privacy-notice. From time to time we may also exchange your personal information with reputable third parties. If you wish to opt out of this sharing of your personal information, please visit readerservice.com/consumerchoice or call 1-800-873-8635. **Notice to California Residents**—Under California law, you have specific rights to control and access your data. For more information on these rights and how to exercise them, visit corporate.harlequin.com/california-privacy.

HDHP23

HARLEQUIN
PLUS

Try the best multimedia
subscription service for romance
readers like you!

Read, Watch and Play.

Experience the easiest way to get
the romance content you crave.

Start your **FREE TRIAL** at
<u>www.harlequinplus.com/freetrial</u>.